AMELIA EARHART
BETRAYED

AMELIA EARHART
BETRAYED

ROBERT WHEELER AND HAROLD NICELY

AMERICAN STRIPES

Amelia Earhart Betrayed

This is a work of fiction. While real individuals
are depicted, their actions here are entirely
the product of the authors' imagination.

Published by American Stripes
351 N. Congress Ave. #115
Boynton Beach, Florida 33426

Flying Pig Media
www.flyingpigmedia.com

Book design by VMC Art & Design LLC

Printed in the United States of America
First Edition, August 2012

ISBN 978-0-9857183-0-5

This book is dedicated
to Amelia Earhart, Frederick Noonan
and to all victims of betrayal,
either by governments
or individuals.

QUOTES BY AMELIA EARHART

"Please know I am quite aware of the hazards. I
want to do it because I want to do it."
From a passage in a letter to her husband,
George Putnam, before leaving on her last flight.

"Women must try to do things as men have
tried. When they fail, their failure must be
but a challenge to others."

"Courage is the price that life exacts for granting
peace with yourself."

"The most effective way to do it,
is to just do it."

AMELIA EARHART
BETRAYED

PREFACE

This world is full of mysteries. What happened to Amelia Earhart and why, is one of the most enduring. Was her disappearance caused by simple navigation error? Was an error made by one of the foremost navigators in the world at the time? Not very likely. Was she on a secret mission for FDR's government? Very likely. Was there a cover-up? If so, by whom and how extensive was it? Whatever it was, Amelia is like gold fever, and once the bug bites it's hard to think of anything else. At first she appears to be a tomboy in her slacks and flannel shirt, quick with a pleasant smile and always a demure lady. A closer look uncovers the truth: She was a driven woman. Her determination and skill were legendary, but these qualities were tempered with patience, charm and above all, knowledge about herself and the aircraft she flew. She was a member of the National Woman's Party and an early supporter of the Equal Rights Amendment. Very close to her heart was the advancement of women in the field of aviation. Amelia had developed a friendship with Eleanor Roosevelt, and had promised to teach her to fly. Mrs. Roosevelt obtained her student pilot's license in anticipation of working with Amelia.

Amelia believed that aviation should not be strictly a man's world simply because women didn't choose to participate because of preconceived notions about women's abilities. Her scrapbook of newspaper clippings about successful women in the fields of law, advertising, management, mechanical engineering, film direction and production was very dear to her. She didn't accept the notion that there were male pursuits and female pursuits; she believed that they were all human pursuits and women were equal to men.

When she received her pilots license on May 15, 1923, mankind had less than 20 years of powered flight experience, women had much less. She was the 16th woman to receive a pilot license. The Federation Aeronautique Internationale issued her license number 6017 (6012 men and 15 women had received licenses previously). Amelia Mary Earhart Putnam and her navigator, Frederick Joseph "Fred" Noonan, took off from Miami Municipal Airport on a marathon flight around the world; A flight that would circumnavigate the globe at it longest point, the equator. This was to be a first in aviation history, never before achieved by anyone, man or woman.

There are 2000 miles unaccounted for on the last leg of her *Around the World Flight*. What did she do for 2000 miles and who did she do it for? Why did the U.S. Navy spend 60 million and change in today's dollars to search for a civilian pilot? These are questions that still beg answers 75 years later. The fate of Amelia Earhart and Fred Noonan was sealed by world politics, government paranoia, the gathering clouds of war and her own bravery in the face of overwhelming odds.

The government's official explanation of her disappearance portrayed Earhart as a helpless female, terrified at the prospect of dying. *She got lost, ran very low on fuel, panicked, lost control of her aircraft and crashed into the deep blue waters of the Pacific, never to be seen again.* Why not put a bow around that neat little package and feed it to the public? That explanation made no sense in 1937 and makes even less sense today. Numerous documents not available in 1937 have shed a great deal of light on the incident. Also, the internet has contributed to the co-ordination of great quantities of data and joint research. The 1937 explanation did, however, serve the purposes of the individuals who had abandoned her. She was a knowledgeable, cool-under-pressure person who wouldn't have panicked, nor lost control of her aircraft under any circumstance. Amelia proved again and again that she had the presence of mind to do what was necessary in an emergency and the ability to make the right decision without emotion. She was the female version of "Sully" in her time. "Sully" Sullenberger will always be remembered as the heroic captain of the airliner whose flight ended without injuries in the Hudson River in NY after losing both engines to a flight of birds.

The around the world flight came at a time in history that was quite difficult. People were not ready to accept another world war, but the fires had already ignited. Hitler had already flown in the face of the Versailles Treaty that ended World War I by reoccupying the Rhineland and introducing military conscription. Spain was in a civil war with Germany backing the Fascists and Russia behind the Communists. The Italians had rolled over Ethiopia. The Japanese had been in a limited war with China since Japan's invasion of Manchuria on September 19, 1931. Japanese troops were threatening the Chinese controlled areas south of Beijing. The United States, France and Britain chose pacification rather than confrontation. They handled the Axis powers with kid gloves because of their fear of another war.

The CIA didn't exist, in fact there was no central agency at all to oversee the gathering of foreign intelligence. As a result the Departments of State, Treasury and War, along with the Army and Navy, ran their own agencies. FDR was in his second term as president and could see that World War was in the near future. Congress was passing laws, mainly the Neutrality Acts, between the two world wars, and were designed to keep the U.S. out of the last war and not the war whose clouds were gathering on the horizon. The intelligence agencies worked only on matters that affected their own special interests. It was up to the chief executive to watch out for the U.S. as a whole.

FDR had been Assistant Secretary of the Navy from 1913 to 1920, answering only to the Secretary of the Navy and helping to implement policies during World War I. It's no secret that he sympathized with Great Britain and France and saw them as a buffer between Germany and Italy and the U.S. He also knew that no such buffer existed between Japan and the U.S.'s interests in the Pacific. He could depend on Britain and France to keep tabs on Europe, but it was his job to keep tabs on Japan. FDR worked tirelessly behind the scenes during the years leading up to the Second World War, doing everything he could to strengthen U.S. armed forces for what he saw as the upcoming conflict.

Secret missions were launched in the Pacific, some succeeded such as the monitoring of Japanese ships using High Frequency Direction Finding and the breaking of the Red and Blue codes, as well as the Magic code. The Magic code was the Japanese equivalent of the German's Enigma code. The Magic code intercepts prior to December, 1941 warning of an attack on US installations were ignored.

Captain Black's forays into the Japanese held Marshalls and Marianas failed, mostly because his intelligence findings were ignored. Captain Black's report detailing an attack on Pearl Harbor by the Japanese on a Sunday in December in 1940 or 1941 was also ignored and we all know the ensuing debacle.

Those were times when people believed what the members of the government said. They also believed that their country was always in the right, that it would *never* do anything underhanded or pull dirty tricks. Today we don't entertain such naïve thoughts. We know that every country has and will continue to do *ANYTHING* it feels necessary to preserve itself. All governments, including the U.S. Government, are made up of people, and people are capable of anything, from the very worst to the very best and everything in between.

It is with these matters in mind that we begin

our story of the round the world flight. Later it was to bear the name *The Final Flight*, detailing the adventures of the world famous aviatrix Amelia Mary Earhart Putnam and her navigator Fredrick Joseph "Fred" Noonan.

Our story is historically correct. We have been meticulous in our research of archives, letters, flight logs, radio logs, books, celestial navigation, flight manuals and performance charts of the *Electra*. We have applied logic in evaluating our research and the research of others. With these facts we have written an account of what happened on that flight, a flight that has lasted 75 years.

Whether you believe our account or not is up to you. Whether there is ever going to be positive proof of what happened to them is up to powers far above any of us. We feel that it's about time that Amelia and Fred got the recognition for their accomplishments, not their failure, and above all their bravery. We hope the right people will see fit to make it possible for them to go to their final rest with the peace and recognition they so richly deserve.

CHAPTER ONE

JULY 2, 1937

100 Miles from Howland Island
in the mid-Pacific Ocean

There they were, finally, the first rays of dawn. The ocean below was still dark, exactly as it had been throughout the long, nerve wracking night. Deep down Amelia Earhart was sure everything would be all right now; dawn had always lifted her spirits. She had just radioed the U.S. Coast Guard Cutter *Itasca* and reported that they were 200 miles out. Then she had whistled into the microphone so that hopefully they could get a radio fix on her. Maybe now someone would talk to her, but that wasn't scheduled to happen until the top of the hour. She rummaged in the bag that she kept beside her seat and found her canteen. The lukewarm water was not refreshing, but at least it quenched her thirst. Whistling into the mic had dried her mouth out. The constant loud drone of the engines, a sound that she usually relished, was beginning to grate on her nerves. It had been almost 18 hours non-stop since they had roared to life on the grass strip that served as the Lae, New Guinea airport. She had been so exhilarated as her overloaded plane, a Lockheed *Electra,* had roared down the runway, her heart beating wildly. Her hands worked the throttles pushing them full forward to make sure she had the full 1200 horsepower pulling the sleek *Electra* down the runway. She eased back on the yoke, the steering wheel, to pull the nose up. This moment was always so exciting, because the end of the runway was racing toward her at 80 miles an hour. On every takeoff when she pulled the yoke smoothly back and the nose lifted into the air, there was a short delay before the wheels left the ground. That short delay was when the adrenaline really started to flow, the stomach knotted and the heart raced. The brain focuses on the myriad things she'd have to do in case the powerful machine won't fly. All senses are heightened the moment the wheels left the ground and she's flying. Then began the work of getting the landing gear and flaps up. Those few moments are what make people want to capture and recapture this natural high. One never tires of the feeling. Her heart had leaped again as they flew over the edge of the cliff at the end of the runway and the azure blue water of the Solomon Sea was suddenly right there, 50 feet below her. The smell of exhaust fumes, mixed with the pungent odor of gasoline, had added so much to her excitement on takeoff. Now they were making her a little light headed.

The light in the eastern sky was getting brighter, making the frothy white caps become visible below. No one had answered her radio calls since she took off from Lae yesterday. Was it yesterday? Or was it day before yesterday? She couldn't be sure. Crossing the International Date Line confuses everyone and she was no exception. She looked in her diary and confirmed to herself they had taken off at 10:00 a.m. on July 1, 1937; yes, it was there in black and white. Glancing at her watch, she realized they had been airborne almost 18 hours and it would be at least another hour and a half before she could close her eyes and get some sleep. Sleep, yes, sweet slumber. Somewhere in the back of her mind she remembered what it was like to shut her eyes for more than a few seconds. She and Fred would be able to close their eyes for a few hours on Howland Island before taking off for Hawaii. Until then she had to remain as sharp as possible, after all, so much depended on this flight, maybe even the future of womankind! She turned in her pilot's seat to look over the fuel tanks behind her at Fred Noonan, her trusted navigator. He had never been more than 2 minutes off in his estimates since they took off from Miami, Florida on June 1st about four week earlier. There was no possible way I could have done this alone. Pity, I always depended on my own ability, but on this trip I needed expert help and Fred was just the man, she reflected as her mind wandered.

Fred didn't look up from his table as he was busy with the business of finding out what went wrong. "Damn it!" swearing under his breath, "Somehow things don't match up and I'm not sure how that happened." He passed Amelia a note telling her they were 200 miles from their destination, Howland Island. Howland was a flat, two mile long, one mile wide fly speck of land in the middle of the Pacific, the largest most desolate ocean in the world. The U.S. Coast Guard Cutter *Itasca* had been dispatched to Howland to act as a homing beacon just for her. When Fred had first signed on with Amelia, he knew that this would be the hardest leg of their fight around the world. Just before they had taken off from Miami, he told some friends, "Finding Howland is going to be like taking off from California in the middle of the night, flying to New York and then looking for a place the size of Central Park. This, after only looking at the ground three times during the entire 19 hour trip." A challenge, to say the least, even for one of the best navigators in the world.

Fred had set up the Pan American Clipper routes from California to Australia. He had been a ship's captain, pilot and navigator. Fred could navigate expertly by the sun, moon, stars and radio beacons, the newest tool of this age-old profession. He had estimated their position to be 200 miles from Howland 20 minutes ago, but the sun was starting to come up. If he had been correct the sun shouldn't rise for another half an hour. His gaze was fixed on the side window, watching the orange ball grow larger, so he could get a sighting. He had first become uncomfortable when they had picked up a 40 mile per hour headwind three hours ago. Amelia had had to increase their airspeed by 20 miles per hour to compensate. She hated to do this because it used more of her precious fuel supply.

Amelia became impatient while waiting for Fred to notice that she was staring at him. When he finally looked up, she shrugged her shoulders, threw up her two hands and shouted, "What's wrong?" over the drone. He held up 5 fingers closed his fist and held up 5 fingers again. "10 minutes?" she mouthed again and he nodded and turned immediately back to his sighting. She knew something was amiss by the tell-tale frown lines on his brow as well as the uncharacteristic beads of sweat dripping down his face onto his shirt. Amelia was exceptionally adept at flying and solving mechanical problems, but she also had a knack for reading people. I know that look, she thought as her neck muscles clenched on her already taut body. Oh, no, it spells trouble. Quickly dissolving was her euphoric feeling, the one that she had felt at the first sign of daybreak reflecting off the beautiful deep blue of the ocean below. The image vanished from her mind as the words of one of her first flight instructors came back to her. "Always make sure that your mind is at least two steps ahead of your hands." She began to calculate how much fuel she had left, something she did every half hour, because fuel was of utmost concern. If there was trouble, fuel would always be a major consideration in her decision. Any uncertainty of their location was just as big a problem. The sun was now becoming a nuisance as it was in her eyes. Feeling around in her bag, she retrieved her sunglasses and put them on to reduce the glare. She went back to her fuel calculations.

Fred's pencil was a blur on his scratch pad. He checked and rechecked his calculations to make sure they were correct. They were now 102 miles from Howland. That would have been excellent news to most pilots and navigators, but he knew that somehow he had erred when he last calculated the winds and their position. "I don't have the time to worry about it now," he softly decided. "There's work to be done." He passed another note up to the cockpit on the end of a bamboo stick that he used for that purpose. Amelia didn't look at all happy when she read, "100 miles from Howland."

"What the hell is going on?" Her shout was drowned out by the engines, but he could read her lips. He shrugged his shoulders and tilted his head to one side, the universal gesture for *beats me*. He wrote another note and passed it forward. "Give me 30 minutes, I'll find out what's up."

"Oh my god!" she whispered after reading the note. "30 minutes is a lifetime." Amelia reduced the throttles and started a slow descent to 4000 feet. She had calculated their remaining fuel and that ole' sick feeling in the pit of her stomach was starting to grow. Paul Mantz, her good friend and instructor had once said, "The only time you have too much fuel is when you're on fire." The fuel gauge needles indicated half a tank in each wing which translated to about 4 hours of flight time. Not a real problem unless you're in the middle of the ocean and the nearest land could be much, much, more than 4 hours away. She looked at her watch after the controls were set. It was only 10 after the hour and she was supposed to transmit only at 15 and 45 minutes past. But, it was important that she call the *Itasca* and let them know something was amiss. Amelia took a deep breath, something she had always done when she was apprehensive since her early childhood in Hutchinson, Kansas. Her voice was steady as she spoke into the mic,

"*Itasca*, KHAQQ calling, take a bearing on us and report on the half hour: I will make noise in the mike…100 miles out." She whistled into the mic for 20 seconds and then reached for her canteen. At that moment she thought that the Sahara wasn't as dry as her mouth.

Fred Noonan's brain was racing and he kept muttering aloud knowing Amelia couldn't possibly hear him. "Where did I make the mistake?" It would be another 30 minutes before he could make another sighting that would tell him about where they were. He checked and rechecked all his wind calculations, but they all proved to be correct. "Maybe I did one of the sightings wrong, but how could that be? I did each one three times just to make sure there was no mistake, yet we aren't where I thought we should be. She won't accept an answer unless I'm 100% positive." They were in a Lockheed *Electra* over the Pacific

Ocean less than 100 miles from where the miniscule island should be. That was the only certainty. Could they have suddenly picked up a 100 mile per hour tail wind? Not very likely, the mistake had to be his.

JULY 2, 1937

Howland Island – mid-Pacific

At 6:20 a.m. Captain Thompson stood on the bridge of the U.S Coast Guard Cutter *Itasca* watching the plume of black smoke rolling from the single stack. He remarked to Lieutenant J.G. Bill Swanston, the deck officer, "That goddamned smoke is dispersing before it reaches 300 feet. She won't be able to see it more than 5 miles away. Tell the engine room to stop making smoke at zero six thirty. I don't want number one boiler clogged with soot."

"Aye, Aye, Sir." He waited for the captain's nod before going into the wheel house to call down to the engine room. "Stop smoke at zero six thirty," practically yelling over the phone. He was beginning to feel the excitement of seeing the most famous woman in the world land at this tiny American outpost. He knew that Howland was the only American possession in the central Pacific that was suitable for building a runway capable of landing the *Electra*. They had brought fuel, aircraft parts and additional parts for the earth movers that the navy kept on the island. The runways had been regraded and repaired by colonists and Hawaiian laborers that were brought here for that purpose. 1st Lieutenant Cooper from the Army Air Corps in Hawaii had been in charge. He had completed all preparations in record time considering that the *Itasca* hadn't arrived at Howland until June 24th. Cooper had reported yesterday that all was ready for the *Electra*'s arrival and Captain Thompson had breathed a visible sigh of relief at the news. Swanston thought he had even smiled, something that didn't happen very often.

Thompson turned away from his gaze to the southwest and barked at Swanston, "Where the hell are you?"

"Right here, sir." Swanston answered from the door of the wheel house.

"Go down to the radio room and find out what's going on."

"Aye, Aye, sir." The young lieutenant was already headed down the steps toward the radio room when he answered.

"Good man," muttered Thompson under his breath as he turned back towards the southwest, his eyes searching the horizon.

The radio room aboard the *Itasca* was very cramped. The room was only large enough for 2 chairs for the three men assigned. There were screen doors at each end for ventilation. The room was located next to the battery room just behind the main stack. Cramped, hot and noisy, not the best work environment. When Swanston arrived for the second time since six o'clock, the two inexperienced operators and their supervisor, Radioman First Class Leo Bellarts, were busy trying to make contact with the Earhart plane.

"Have you heard anything?" questioned Swanston.

"We received her last call just before sun-up. She was 200 miles out and whistling into the mic." Leo Bellarts didn't look too enthused about the young lieutenant's interruption. He had received word that Frank Cipriani, manning the high frequency direction finder on Howland, was very frustrated. Earhart hadn't transmitted long enough for him to get a bearing on her, so his report reflected the disappointing news. Tension was beginning to grow, both in the radio room and on shore.

Swanston left just before 6:30 a.m. and hurried back to the bridge to report to Captain Thompson whose only comment was, "Damn it, why won't she transmit on 500 kilocycles so we can track her?"

Swanston looked a little sheepish when he answered, "I don't know, sir."

"I didn't expect you to, lieutenant, didn't expect you to!" His glance, which usually froze young lieutenants in their tracks, was somehow not as stern. Maybe he was just getting tired, thought Swanston.

"It looks like they've stopped making smoke; I need a cup of coffee." His look was back to its usual lieutenant-freezing best. Swanston knew that he was already late with the coffee. When he returned with a steaming mug, he was greeted with, "Get back down to the radio room and find out what's up."

"Aye, Aye, sir." Swanston was already on his way. When he squeezed into the already over-crowded room he saw Bellarts standing next to his radio with an astonished look on his face that was caused by the last call received from Earhart. "What's happened?" Swanston asked.

"Sir, she has covered 100 miles in the 27 minutes since she last reported! That seems impossible, I didn't know the plane would go that fast."

"I wouldn't know, but it sounds pretty fast to me." Swanston backed out of the door because there wasn't enough space to turn around, and ran to the bridge.

She hadn't answered a single one of their calls and they had responded to every one of hers. Head operator, Leo Bellarts, had tried in vain to make contact. He was supposed to transmit to her in Greenwich Mean Time (used as the basis for standard time throughout most of the world) because that's what Amelia was using. But because his commander refused to switch to Greenwich Mean Time (GMT), he had to convert local time to GMT before he made each call. The captain wanted constant up-to-the-minute briefings, so Lieutenant Swanston was in and out every ten to fifteen minutes. Coast Guard Headquarters in San Francisco was calling every 15 minutes requesting an update. The other two operators, William Galten and Thomas O'Hare, were too inexperienced to know what to do in a critical situation like this. The relief operator, Gilbert Thompson, was also just as new to the job. Headquarters was constantly asking questions. So, Bellarts, as the only knowledgeable man in the room, was becoming overwhelmed with the constant interference from outside sources, not to mention the over-heated and claustrophobic conditions. Consequently, now when Amelia needed their help most, the men in the radio room lost track of the scheduled times to transmit and receive. Amelia and the radiomen wound up transmitting at the same time. Tragically for Amelia, this meant they couldn't hear each other. As is usual with most emergencies, when things get tense, people start to fall apart. Sadly, this is precisely when cool heads should prevail.

JULY 2, 1937

Kwajalein Atoll - Tokkeitai Headquarters (Japanese Naval Secret Police)

The Tokkeitai compound was on the east side of the atoll about 100 yards from the beach. It consisted of seven single story wooden buildings on stilts. The entire compound was enclosed on three sides by a high wall, topped with two strands of electric wire. The beach side had only an electrified wire fence. The radio intercept section was in one end of Hut 2. The section personnel were monitoring Amelia's frequency. Navy Lieutenant Commander Ohayashi, Officer in Charge, was being updated as each intercept was received. Ohayashi had stepped outside to watch the early morning dawn, one of his favorite times of the day. Because the gentle breakers on the beach were visible he guessed the time should be about 15 after 6 o'clock. He turned, walked back into the hut and looked at the clock. 6:16, not a bad guess, he thought egotistically. He was taking a drink from his canteen when the radio crackled to life. "Earhart calling *Itasca*, please take a bearing on 3105 on the hour, will whistle in the microphone about 200 miles out approximately, whistling now.

"Very strange, her asking for a bearing on such a high frequency, I wonder if she meant 500 kilocycles? What do you think Sato?"

Lieutenant Commander Sato was the head of the Intelligence Section located in the other half of Hut 2. He had been back and forth between his own office and the radio intercept section since they got the emergency alert about the incident at Truk Atoll. "I don't know, but it would seem to require further investigation, maybe after this situation is resolved?"

"I think you're right. She is only 200 miles from Howland and it looks like she is going to slip through our fingers."

"It would appear so..."Sato's voice trailed off as he looked at the clock on the wall. He was beginning to fear that they would never intercept Amelia's aircraft. "You're exactly right, I think. A pity, she probably has spoiled many years of hard work."

Ohayashi's face showed his concern. "Do you have any suggestions?"

"Pray for a miracle, our only hope is that she won't find Howland Island."

"I'm afraid that hope is almost gone. She is only two hundred miles from her destination and doesn't seem to be concerned about finding the island.

Sato's face darkened as he realized how hopeless the situation was becoming. "Let me know if there is any change, I have other matters to attend to," Sato said over his shoulder as he left the room.

Ohayashi went back to listening to the radio. He understood what she was saying because he spoke English, only school English. That's because he hadn't been educated in the United States. Many of his contemporaries had been selected to attend a university in America, but he had been too valuable in his present position to spare for any length of time. The same was true of Sato.

Sato walked to Hut 7 in the northeast corner of the compound. It was surrounded by an electrified fence with a gate in the front. A guard at the gate snapped to attention when Sato entered. The 3 enlisted men in the front room jumped to attention when Sato opened the door.

"Let's get this over with!" His voice was an order.

One of the men slung his rifle over his shoulder as he walked to a locked door at the far end of the hut. The two young sailors in the locked room got to their feet when the key turned in the lock, so they were standing when the door opened. They both snapped to attention when Sato appeared at the door and pointed to one of them. The chosen prisoner turned pale as he stood waiting and Sato motioned for him to come out of the room. Both of the prisoners looked as if they had been questioned rather brutally. The area around their eyes was black and blue and several cuts were apparent on their faces. The selected man was missing 3 fingernails on his right hand and the bloody ends indicated they had been yanked out very recently. The other man was missing the thumb and forefinger on his left hand. They had obviously been lopped off within the last two days.

Take him outside and tie him to a pole!" Sato ordered.

Two of the guards walked the prisoner outside and tied him to one of the two poles standing between the back of the building and the beach. Sato watched the guard lock the other prisoner up and walked outside.

"You're lucky, you confessed and we are in the process of arresting the other members of your group. The other prisoner didn't talk, so his death will not be as easy as yours." Sato spoke in low even tones. He drew his pistol and with a very fluid motion raised it and shot the man in the side of the head. The man's head snapped to the left and fell forward. His legs buckled and he slumped. Sato had been careful to shoot him so that nothing got on the pole.

"Feed him to the sharks," Sato ordered. The two guards cut the man loose letting him fall to the ground. They then dragged him by the feet to the gate where the third guard had a truck waiting. The limp body was unceremoniously dumped into the back of the truck and they drove off to the Tokkeitai "cemetery". A pier jutted out into a calm, very blue ocean that shimmered in the sunlight. This beautiful scene was briefly interrupted as the body made a resounding splash. Within two minutes the cruising sharks moved in for a short feeding frenzy and devoured the lifeless body. The three guards knew that within the next couple of days the man left in Hut 7 would also end up there, but he would be tied hand and foot and still alive.

While Sato was taking care of business, Ohayashi had heard Amelia's last call. He had just finished some quick calculations when Sato came in.

"She made another call; she's 100 miles from Howland. 100 miles in 27 minutes, I just figured it out, that is 205 miles per hour. No wonder our planes couldn't catch her. Our information was that she normally flies at 140 miles per hour."

Sato looked somewhat puzzled and finally said, "It doesn't change anything, she gave us the slip and there will be hell to pay when the brass gets hold of it. I'm sure somehow it will be our fault. Not doing our job, you know."

Ohayashi nodded in agreement. A woman pilot had not only flown over Truk Atoll, but probably had taken pictures of their super-secret installations. And the final insult, she had managed to evade their fighters. Very embarrassing to say the least, especially in a country like Japan where women did not garner the respect they enjoyed in other countries. After all, this was 1937.

Paul Mantz, Amelia Earhart, Paul Manning, and Fred Noonan.

CHAPTER
TWO

JULY 2, 1937

Howland Island

Amelia coaxed the throttles forward and stopped her slow, lazy descent at 4000 feet. "Ah, prop pitch, just a hair less, that's it old girl, a little bit more." She was talking quietly to her plane as they were like one entity. She knew Fred couldn't hear, and it didn't matter if he could, anyway. She adjusted the controls. "Let everything stabilize, like you were taught and then make the fine adjustments." Her voice was drowned out by the constant drone of the engines. She looked back over the tanks to see if Fred had made any progress. "I wonder how many people could sit for 18 hours and not go crazy: my butt is killing me, my shoulders ache and as much as I love flying, this is a little too much." Her gut was tight with tension and has been ever since she realized that Fred had made a mistake.

Fred made his sighting once, twice, three times as was his method. He couldn't afford another mistake;

the last one was bad enough. As usual his pencil virtually flew over the paper.

"Damn it quit thinking about how this happened and FIX IT!" He yelled it so loud that Amelia whirled around and stared at him. "What the hell? That can't be right, we were right on course 3 hours ago." He began his calculations all over again. "We couldn't be that far south. Not in a million years could that happen!"

"Continue on this course? What the hell is going on? Where are we?" She was glaring at him, yelling at him to make herself heard over the drone, or maybe just good old fashioned anger. Fred scribbled another note. "It looks like we might be a degree or two off course. I'll know better in 10 more minutes." He went back to figuring instead of meeting her glaring stare. He kept his next revelations to himself. She was gentle as a lamb, until there was a problem, then the gloves came off and she knew how to kick ass, boy, did she know how to kick ass.

As was her usual practice when things got really stressful, she would go over what led up to this moment. Just a little less RPM on number one engine and they will be in sync. She always took care of the business at hand first. The synchronized drone of the engines made it easier for her to relax and think back to the start of her around the world trip.

MARCH 17, 1937

Three and one-half months earlier
Oakland, California

It was about four in the afternoon on St. Patrick's Day when she had coaxed the twin engine *Electra* off the runway at Oakland, California and climbed towards the Golden Gate Bridge. She had stretched her neck a little to get a better look at the famous landmark. The grey rain clouds were quickly breaking up so the afternoon sun could create a light show on the bay. A freighter was just passing under the bridge as she soared toward her cruising altitude. On the advice of Paul Mantz, her co-pilot, she leveled off at 3500 feet. Paul was Amelia's friend and mentor. He had asked her if it was all right if he could go along on this flight to Honolulu to get to Hawaii as quickly as possible. His future bride was bound for America's paradise on the USS *Malolo* that would dock in Honolulu tomorrow. He wanted to meet her and this, according to him, was the fastest way to the islands.

She was thinking about that request and how it was that's just an excuse. I know you wanted to make sure everything went smoothly on this leg. Friends worry about friends, but Paul, you aren't the type to let anyone know that you are a little concerned. I'll let you think I believe your feeble excuse. She chuckled to herself and smiled at him as he adjusted the engine RPM's and added a little prop pitch. The thought had amused her; she was also pleased with herself because he didn't have the slightest idea why she was smiling at him.

Fred Noonan and Paul Manning were in the back of the fuel-ladened *Electra*. Manning was a very experienced pilot, ship's captain and navigator. He was happy and honored to act as co-navigator on this leg of her journey. They both were taking sightings and scribbling on paper pads. Amelia had the best team she could ask for on this leg of her journey. Between Noonan and Manning, they knew exactly where they were every second of the 15 hour and 48 minute flight. Paul Mantz landed the aircraft at Wheeler Field at 5:55 a.m. Hawaii time. Amelia put on her usual smiling face for the crowd that had gotten up so early to greet them. Spectators and reporters crowded around the intrepid quartet, asking questions and taking pictures, Radio announcers were excitedly describing what they saw and trying to get a few words from one of the four celebrities. Amelia gave a short report about the flight. Afterwards she thought, I can't believe I lied so well when I said the flight was uneventful and the aircraft performed perfectly. It had happened just exactly as it had before. When I was in Oklahoma in February on my way to California, the pitch control on the right propeller had stuck. Neither of us were able to move it. This wasn't a horrible problem unless my left engine quit. (This meant that she wouldn't be able to get full power out of the right engine. It's like going up a hill in high gear. When the car slows, the driver should shift down to a lower gear in order to maintain speed and continue to climb the hill. If a person cannot downshift, then the car will get slower and slower until it won't make it up the incline.) I didn't want to go to all the trouble to explain that to them. All they wanted to hear was how everything went well, so that's what I told them.

Amelia, who obviously headed the group, designated Paul Mantz as her technical representative and put him in full charge of getting the aircraft ready for next leg of the flight. She handled the press and spectators while Mantz and Lt. Donald Arnold, the engineering officer at the near-by Luke airfield, went about the business of getting the *Electra* ready to make the hop to Howland Island as soon as possible.

MARCH 2, 1937

Four months earlier
Department of the Navy, Washington, D.C.

In 1937 very few people in the U.S. knew about the Office of Naval Intelligence (ONI) as it was nicely hidden from public view in a division of the Navy's Bureau of Navigation. Many Washington insiders, as well as the general population, had no reason to know about the workings of the premiere foreign intelligence-gathering organization in the U.S. Government. ONI was responsible for the protection of naval personnel and censorship. It also consisted of a large network of counter-intelligence personnel who tracked and uncovered enemy spies and saboteurs. They also provided the Navy with the intelligence necessary to plan strategy in order to counter threats by other naval powers: in 1937 that was primarily the Japanese.

Commander Edward Lanning was described

by his superiors and contemporaries as a human dynamo. He was sharp, quick-thinking, fast acting, intuitive, adept at comprehension and extremely aggressive: the perfect man for the job at hand. Much had happened three weeks before Amelia's take-off from Oakland. He was summoned to the Assistant Chief of The Bureau of Navigation's office. Even though he was 15 minutes early he was ushered in immediately upon his arrival. Must be damned important, everyone has to wait at least a half hour after the appointment time, he thought. He was cordially greeted and invited to sit down.

"Lanning, are you aware of the flight around the world being made by Amelia Earhart?

"Yes sir, I am"

"We need her to do a mission for us and I think you're the man for the job of convincing her."

"What mission, sir?"

"The Japs are fortifying Truk Atoll, we are sure of it. They've been at it for years and we haven't been able to get anyone there on the ground to take a look. Their security is tight, very tight."

"I'm aware of that sir; I just looked over the League of Nations reports. The Japs are shipping enough rice to Truk to feed an army and no one seems to care."

"We care, Lanning, we care a great deal. Earhart

is flying the wrong way, she's going east to west, and we've got to get her started the other way."

"That's not gonna be easy, sir."

"That's why I called you; if it was easy I could get anybody to do it."

"Yes sir, any restrictions on what I can do."

"Just one, try not to kill anyone and if you have to, make sure it isn't her."

"Yes sir, anything else?"

"Yes, this operation is very secret. It comes directly from Pennsylvania Avenue and as few people as possible are to know anything about it. There is one more thing that you should know: no one but you and I are to know the *complete* plan. See my secretary on the way out, she has a file on what has been done so far. Good luck, a lot is riding on this one, no screw-ups."

"I'll do my best sir." Lanning then turned and left the office.

Betty Chapel, a no nonsense Texan, like her boss, handed him a rather thin folder when he came out of the boss's office. "Is this all there is?" He didn't catch himself in time before asking the question.

"Commander Lanning, what do you think? This is it, all we have. Good day…Sir!"

Her displeasure at being questioned was very apparent.

"Good Day Mrs. Chapel."

His mind was racing with plans during the 30-minute drive back to his office. First, she had to be stopped before she gets any further than Hawaii. Lanning always did things step by step and step one was stating the problem. He wasn't one of those people who tried to find a solution without a clear understanding of exactly what the problem was.

The file contained the usual personal information and photos, mostly from the newspapers. He read everything that was there and looked for more. Damnation, we bought her that airplane. There it is in black and white: $80,000 dollars to Perdue University for the *Electra* and a copy of the letter to the president of the college. He quickly scanned the documents and knew what to do.

"Joan, get me Kelly Johnson at Lockheed." Johnson was the chief engineer at Lockheed Aircraft Corporation in Burbank, California.

"Yes sir."

A few minutes later Joan's voice came over the intercom on his desk. "Mr. Johnson on the line for you, sir."

"Thanks Joan, also get me whatever you can on a Paul Mantz and Paul Manning."

"Yes sir."

"Hello Kelly, how are you this fine day?"

"I was doing all right until just a minute ago, what can I do for you?"

"I need to meet with you. I'm flying out to the west coast tonight. Is day after tomorrow at 9 okay?"

"Do I have a choice?"

"Not if you want Lockheed to continue to build planes for the Navy."

"Nine A.M it is, then. Anything else?"

"Yes, make sure Paul Mantz is there."

"I'll do my best, Bye"

"Bye Kelly, sweet dreams."

Johnson didn't hear the last part of the conversation. He had hung up and was looking for Paul Mantz's phone number. Kelly knew that if you didn't play ball with ONI you didn't get Navy contracts; it was as simple as that.

At 9 a.m. sharp, two days later, Lanning was escorted into Kelly Johnson's office. Paul Mantz sat in one of the red leather chairs in front of Kelly's desk. He stood as Lanning entered the room.

"Paul this is..." Lanning had held his finger to his lips.

"The Man from ONI will do very nicely, thank you"

"Yes, of course..."

Mantz nodded his head and shook Lanning's hand and they all sat down.

"Mr. Mantz…"

"Paul, Please."

"Paul, then, it's my understanding you are very adept at aerial photography and long distance flying; you are also a stunt pilot."

"I'm not a stunt pilot, sir, I'm a precision pilot."

"I appreciate the distinction; Paul we need your help."

"What can I do?"

"Teach Amelia Earhart everything you can about photography and long distance flying."

"When? She won't be back from her around the world flight till the end of April or the first of May, I don't think I can do it before then."

Lanning's stiffened, "She'll return before that, it's is being arranged as we speak."

Suddenly Mantz was very curious as he knew that this was extremely important to Amelia. This guy, this Man from ONI, was saying she wasn't going to make it? "What do you mean by that?"

"In my line of work, Mr. Mantz, all information is on a need to know basis, and you don't have a need to know.

Mantz's face reddened and his fists unconsciously balled up as anger swelled up inside of him, "What the hell is that supposed to mean, she's a friend, a very dear friend and I……"

"Paul, drop it!" Kelly Johnson's abrupt words were final and Mantz reluctantly left the question hanging."

"Your job, Mr. Mantz, will be to show Miss Earhart all she needs to know about long distance flying and aerial photography, without regard to its use in the future. What you don't know won't hurt you. What you do know could hurt her, am I understood?"

"Yes, Commander." Lanning noted Mantz's scowl and made a mental note to keep an eye on him in the future. He seemed to have a temper which made him a loose cannon on this mission.

"Mr. Johnson, your job is to get the airplane ready for the mission; here is a list of modifications. Payment will be as usual. Are there any questions gentlemen?" He waited for a reply and when none came, he matter-of-factly said, "I don't need to tell you that this meeting doesn't go beyond this room."

Mantz nodded in agreement as Johnson looked up from the modifications list and replied, "As per usual, Commander." Lanning left the office and neither man looked at the other as they both had their own concerns. Johnson focused on the aircraft and Mantz on Amelia. They both had the utmost respect for Amelia and were extremely fond of her. But this guy, Lanning, if that was his real name, didn't. Mantz knew he had to intervene, but how?

MARCH 18, 1937

10042 Valley Spring Lane
North Hollywood, California

George Putnam was sitting in the living room of the
North Hollywood home that he and his wife, Amelia,
shared. His mind kept drifting as he sat relaxing with

his first cup of coffee before getting to the day's work. Today was a big day for the both of them. He remembered the wonderful time they had at the Waikiki Beach home of Chris and Mona Holmes back in 1935. Paul Mantz had been there also with his first wife. He thought that Paul would probably enjoy this visit with the Holmes, too. This time Paul would be there with his new fiancé, Terry Minor. Chris Holmes was heir to the Fleishmann Yeast fortune. Mona, Chris's wife, was the daughter of a senator that had contributed a great deal to Amelia's exploits. But, this was the depression and nobody's financial bottom line was rosy… His thoughts were interrupted when the phone rang.

"Hello."

"Hello, Geo…" The operator interrupted her, "One moment please Miss." Her tone was cold and impersonal. "I have a collect call for Mr. George Putnam from Miss Amelia Earhart, will you accept the charges."

"Of course I will. Hello darling."

"Hello sweetheart, to get quickly to the point, I love and miss you. The flight went exceptionally well. We arrived at Wheeler Field at approximately 6 o'clock, about 8 o'clock your time. How is everything on your end?"

"Very good, actually. There is one thing that we need to discuss before this flight goes any further."

"What's that?"

"They reported on the radio that Paul Mantz had landed the airplane in Honolulu, is that true."

"Yes, but…" He knew she was frowning at the implication.

"I know that this sounds trite, but remember when you flew with your mechanic. The newspapers claimed that he was really flying the airplane, not you."

"I know dear but that doesn't matter much now, this is my last flight and they will say what they will say."

"I think it would be better if you were alone in the cockpit during takeoffs and landings.

"All right George, can we discuss something else."

He thought her voice was a little strained but this wasn't the best connection in the world. "Amelia, I only want you to be the most famous aviator in the world. Is that too much to ask for?"

"Sometimes you're a little exasperating, George. What possible difference could it make if this reporter or that reporter got it wrong? Because you aren't a woman, George, you have a hard time understanding what we go through. We are used to getting little or no credit for what we do. That is, unless it's something bad, then we get all the credit.'

"I'm sorry dear, tell me about the flight."

"I'm going to talk to Fred about staying with the

flight until Australia. He is really something, George. He can take a celestial fix and tell me our position in *6 minutes.* That's incredible!"

"If you say so dear."

"He has developed some method that lets him do that in a jiffy. It usually takes a ship's navigator 30 minutes to make the same calculation. He told me to slow down, slow down, can you imagine? He knew to the minute when we would sight Diamond Head and if I hadn't slowed down, like he said, we would have arrived before dawn. We averaged a 13 mph tailwind. I also used the direction finder. Now that is a piece of equipment! There I go, sweetheart, on and on about what I'm doing. What have you been doing?"

"Not anything as exciting as what you have been up to. I am getting things ready for your triumphant return to the states. Ticker tape parades, parties, dress balls, you know, all the things you don't like."

"Sounds good, my dear, you keep up that end and I will do my part here. Oh, Paul Mantz just got a call from the airfield, maybe it will be good news. I will talk to you again when I can, I love you."

"I love you too, Amelia," And then she was gone. I hope everything is all right, she didn't mention Paul Manning; I wonder if there is a problem? He put those thoughts aside and went to the kitchen for another cup of coffee. Coffee, what would I do without it? George wouldn't have been so lackadaisical if he had known what Paul Mantz had just found out at the air-field. In fact he would have been downright panicky.

CHAPTER THREE

MARCH 18, 1937

Luke Field on Ford Island
Pearl Harbor, Hawaii

Paul Mantz had good reason to be disturbed when he returned to Wheeler Field that afternoon. Lieutenant Rogers, the station engineering officer at Wheeler Field, 75th Service Squadron, had told Mantz that while servicing the right propeller hub his mechanics had found that it was nearly dry. The mechanics had brought this to the attention of the maintenance foreman, Sergeant Biando. Biando had carefully checked around the hub and found no evidence that the grease had leaked out. He had the mechanics pump the hub full of grease in the hopes that would solve the problem. Mr. Thomas, the representative from Pratt and Whitney, the company that had manufactured the aircraft's engines, felt that the propeller hub had been almost dry when they left Oakland. Lt. Rogers and Lt. Arnold, the engineering officer at near-by Luke Field, also concurred. Mantz decided to run the engines and see for himself if the problem was fixed. While he went through the starting procedure the conversation with the Man from ONI ran through his mind.

"She won't be back from her around the world flight until the end of April or the first of May," Mantz had stated. "She'll return before that, it's being arranged as we speak," the man had corrected. Mantz had questioned the remark at the time and been told to drop the matter by Kelly Johnson.

The two Pratt and Whitney engines roared to life and he ran them through the run-up tests. Everything checked out except he still couldn't change the pitch in the right prop, it was frozen solid. "Those dirty bastards, they sabotaged her aircraft!" he hissed. This upset him as the enormity of their actions started to dawn on him for the first time.

He shut down the engines and when he conferred with everyone, they decided to remove both props in the hopes of solving this mysterious problem. He asked Lt. Arnold to take the props to the Hawaiian Air Depot at Luke Field and have them overhauled. Arnold had already made preparations for just such a request. Mantz had felt satisfied with the arrangements.

He joined Terry, his fiancée, and the others at Chris' that evening. He had seen to all the problems that he could control, but Amelia knew him well enough to know that something wasn't right. I wonder what's wrong with Paul, he seems preoccupied. She stopped abruptly, wondering if she had said that out loud. I guess not, no one is looking over here.

"How's the airplane, Paul?"

"They should have the props ready to go by dawn, or at least that's what I was told. You should be able to leave tomorrow morning."

"Is everything else okay?"

"Just fine," he bluffed, but the forced smile gave a strange appearance to his thin, Errol Flynn style mustache and he was looking away when he spoke directly to her. These signs were all Amelia needed to tell her Paul wasn't himself. Soon, however, the magic of the islands took over. They all had a light dinner with the beautiful Hawaiian night as a backdrop. Soft, moist breezes tickled the palm leaves on the tall tropical trees. The moon was shimmering on the water as the gentle breakers lapped on Waikiki Beach. The cares of day seemed to vanish as Paul enjoyed the pleasures of the moment. Disturbing the mood, the maid came in to announce, "There is a call for you, Mr. Mantz, from a Lieutenant Arnold at Luke Field." Paul excused himself and went to the phone in Chris' study. "Hello?"

"Mr. Mantz, Lt. Arnold here. The right prop was in such terrible condition that we decided to overhaul both props just to be safe. If everything goes well they both should be back to Wheeler at two in the morning and Sergeant Biando assures me the aircraft should be ready to fly by dawn.

"Very good, Lieutenant, thank you very much for all your help. I will make the proper arrangements with Standard Oil. Good night and thanks again."

"You're welcome sir, just doing my job."

Mantz coordinated with Standard Oil so that the *Electra* would be fueled at Wheeler Field the next morning. He still had a bad feeling that even the beauty of the Hawaiian night couldn't dispel.

That night Old Man Weather tortured them with a long, hard, ground soaking downpour. When they all got up at 4:30 the next morning, Paul immediately announced, "I'm afraid the runway at Wheeler Field will be too soft to get your overloaded airplane off the ground successfully."

"Let's go take a look and then we can make a decision," Amelia countered hopefully.

Paul agreed, he was still agitated by the thought that someone had tampered with the aircraft and not a little worried that something else was wrong that he hadn't discovered yet.

Less than an hour later Amelia and Paul were driving down the grass runway at Wheeler Field and they decided after just a few minutes that the *Electra* would never make it off this strip fully loaded with fuel. They returned to Waikiki and Paul invited Terry and Chris to accompany him on the test flight later that morning. Both were happy and excited with the prospect of an adventure. Neither of them had seen a beautiful Pacific island from the air before.

After adding just enough fuel for the test flight, Mantz, Chris and Terry took off for a tour of the entire island and what a tour it was. Paul's passengers were duly impressed with the breath-taking lushness of the foliage, clear water and rocky terrain seen from such heights.

Paul landed at Luke field and congratulated Lieutenants Rogers and Arnold on the excellent work their organizations had done. "Especially thank Sergeant Biando for his part."

"You can do that yourself, he and his whole crew are here to take care of the *Electra*." Lt. Rogers was beaming as he spoke. He pointed towards the final assembly hangar where Biando and his whole crew stood.

"You guys did a fantastic job. Thank you for your extra efforts on Miss Earhart's part."

"Beg your pardon, sir. We do the same for her as we do for all our pilots, they deserve the best. It's quite a responsibility and we take it very seriously. But thanks for the pat on the back, everyone here appreciates it."

"Your pilots are very lucky to have you, thanks again."

He went back later in the day to address some refueling questions and decided that Standard Oil's fuel didn't meet standards. Lt. Arnold refueled the *Electra* from the Army's fuel supply and at 7:30 p.m. Mantz *carefully* watched as the plane was pushed into the hangar, which was then securely locked. He had posted a guard to make sure no one could tamper with the plane before Amelia took off the next morning.

. . . .

All precautions had been taken to make sure no one got into the hangar that night, but no effort had been made to make sure that no one was already in there when it was locked up. At 1:00 o'clock in the morning, when the guard was less observant than he had been before midnight, Jim McNichol left his hiding place in a storage room in the back of the hanger. He could easily see the *Electra* in the moonlight that glowed through the dirty windows panes that were sitting high on the curved walls of the cavernous aircraft storage facility. There was no need for a give-a-way beam of light from a flashlight. In less than 45 minutes he had taken the right main landing gear tire off and removed it from the rim. From his pocket he removed a match box sized container which contained a device that looked like a large capsule. It was a specially made two-part capsule developed by the slick lab technicians at ONI. Upon take-off, when the tire reached 40 mph the centrifugal force would break the membrane between the two parts of the capsule. At the moment the membrane disintegrated, there would be intense heat as the two chemicals collided. This, the experts told him, would be enough to blow the tire. He put some glue on the inside of the tire and then set the tiny device in place. He put the tire back on the rim and mounted it on the *Electra*. His handiwork was well-hidden. The entire operation was complete by 3:00 a.m., so he went into the locker where he had hidden during the day and went to sleep.

. . . .

It was 3:30 the next morning when Chris drove the group through the deserted streets of Honolulu on the way to Pearl Harbor. They boarded the boat bound for the Fleet Airbase Dock on Ford Island. It had rained again and even now it was still misting. They walked to the weather shack to get the latest forecast. There would be a 15 mph tail wind which seemed to delight everyone except Fred Noonan, Amelia's trusted navigator.

"Amelia, do you still want it to be possible to fly back to Honolulu eight hours into the flight?"

"Yes, Fred, I think that is essential."

"You need to consider that the 15 mph tail wind will become a 15 mph head wind on the way back, it will add approximately 2 hours to our flight time if we find it necessary to turn around."

"Excellent point Fred, I'm glad you decided to accompany us to Australia. I hope Mary is okay with it."

"I'm sure she is."

"Paul, would you get them to put on another 75 gallons of fuel?"

"Will do." He left the shack and headed for the final assembly hangar. Amelia, Fred and Paul Manning followed 10 minutes later.

Amelia greeted Lts Rogers and Arnold and Sergeant Biando. "My goodness, none of your people have had a moments rest."

"Thank you Miss Earhart, everyone here volunteered and we are all glad to help as best we can."

She chatted pleasantly with them and talked about some mechanical aspects of her aircraft and her upcoming flight around the world. They were impressed with her knowledge and found her both charming and unassuming. They were pleasantly surprised to find those qualities in such a world-renowned celebrity. At five foot seven and one-half inches, she was tall for a woman of her time. From a distance, she could have been mistaken for one of the mechanics as she dressed in flannel shirts and men's trousers. The press began to arrive at about 4:45 and she politely, but regrettably excused herself from their comfortable conversation. She steeled herself for the predicable questions about how she felt and the trip itself. It wouldn't do to insult the press, so she reminded herself to smile for the cameras and pose as daintily as a tom-boy could.

By 5:00 a.m. the aircraft was fueled and Mantz was going over the plane trying to find the slightest problem. He had missed the grease in the right prop hub in Oakland, so what he could possibly miss now was beginning to haunt him. When he was satisfied with the visual inspection he did a run up check and ran the engines for five minutes to warm them up.

Amelia finished talking to the press and walked to the *Electra*. "Thanks so much Paul, for everything. Relax and enjoy your vacation with Terry, I will be fine. Fred is a first class navigator and Paul Manning is a wiz with the radios. See you back in California."

"Remember the strip is still wet. If you have to brake hard you may slide. Good Luck!"

She had walked up the wing and waved at everyone before she entered through the hatch on the roof of the cockpit. She asked for the flood lights to be turned on so she would have enough light to take off. After the lights were turned on, she decided to wait for more daylight. After all, she was the pilot and made all the decisions based on the advice she was given, but 99% of her actions would be based on her past training, flying experiences and, of course, her unerring instincts.

Noonan and Manning got aboard. At 5:30 a.m. Amelia started her engines and ten minutes later she taxied for takeoff. Mantz walked outside ahead of the tip of the left wing with his flashlight while a mechanic from Depot Maintenance walked in front of the right wing tip. They were both guiding the aircraft with their flashlights as the dim light of dawn began to appear. The sky was surprisingly bright in the direction of the mouth of Pearl Harbor, as she swung the tail around and lined up a little to the right of the runway centerline. She would have felt better with Paul Manning, an experienced pilot, in the right seat but she took George's advice and was alone in the cockpit. The airbase fire truck would drive on the right parallel taxiway so it could remain close in case of an emergency. It would accelerate and keep pace with her plane. Amelia eased the throttles forward to the half-way point before she released the brakes.

The stage was set and the large crowd of spectators and well-wishers held a collective breath. They were witnessing an historic event. It's not every day that they get to see a woman, or man for that matter, break a world record! No one had ever tried to circumnavigate the entire world at it largest girth: by following the equator. The aircraft began its takeoff roll as she brought the engines to their full throttle position. As she did, Mantz and the mechanic stepped to the side of the runway to avoid the prop blast. The roar in the cockpit was deafening, but to Amelia this sound was exhilarating.. She applied full left rudder to the pedal control; this to keep the plane straight on its path: the center line of the runway. The plane, overweight with fuel, was about to fly into history and Mantz felt his chest tighten with dread, instead of expectancy. With a mixture of regret and confusion he watched his friend and student lumber down the runway and he thought, maybe I should have told her. But, he was duty-bound by the government to keep silent: an age old struggle, friendship vs. allegiance to one's country.

Amelia had the control yoke slightly aft (back) to keep

the tail wheel on the ground as the aircraft accelerated. She held her left foot hard on the rudder and her leg was fully extended, but the *Electra* began to drift slightly right of the runway centerline. She reduced the throttle to the left engine ever so little to straighten the nose, and then brought the control yoke to the neutral position. When the tail wheel came off the ground the full weight of the *Electra* shifted to the main gear. She was at 45 mph and everything seemed normal. A split second later the right tire began to leak badly which caused the aircraft to drift further right. She reduced the power a little more on the left engine as she struggled to keep the nose straight; she had no choice until the left rudder took full effect. Now the tire blew out completely! The right wing dropped and the left wing rose. Because she had full left rudder applied, her reaction was to reduce power further on the left engine to continue her efforts at straightening her path down the runway. This is precisely what she should have done. With full left rudder, left engine power reduced and the right tire completely blown the aircraft veered left because the right engine was at full power. Before she could reduce power on the right engine the situation became critical. The left wheel was off the ground with all the weight on the right gear strut. Suddenly the right gear strut collapsed and the wing hit the ground! Corrective action was useless.

All that she could do was ride it out and hope for the best. The entire sequence of events had taken less than 10 seconds. Amelia moved the Magneto switches on both engines to off, shutting them down and reducing the chance of fire. Nine hundred gallons of highly flammable aviation fuel and engine sparks don't mix well at all. Seconds later the *Electra* came to rest with the nose pointed generally back towards their starting point.

She turned around and breathlessly asked her navigators, "Fred, Paul are you all right?"

"I am but I think Paul hurt his elbow." Fred's voice was steady

"Thank God, can you get out of the back?"

"Paul and I are all right, can you get out all right?"

"Yes!" Thank God again for no fire and no one injured, was her thought as she stood up in her seat and pushed herself onto the roof. She jerked her head around as the fire truck almost slid into the right wing, its tires losing traction on the wet runway. Spectators and reporters crowded around the crippled plane and began firing questions. The right wing was damaged and both landing gears were collapsed. The propellor blades were curled at the ends and some of the engine cowling (cover) was missing. The round the world flight was not going to take place until the plane was repaired.

Ever quick to react, Paul Mantz had already begun

to pull bags from the stricken *Electra* before Amelia had left the cockpit. He breathed a sigh of relief that only the airplane was hurt and none of the crew. His mind filled immediately with paranoid queries. How the hell did they do it, or did they do it? Could the Man from ONI have pulled this off?

Amelia was never quite sure if the accident had been pilot error as Mantz contended, or as she thought a blown tire. History has not proved either to be true.

Now it was Kelly Johnson's turn to do his job at the Lockheed plant at Burbank, California and get the *Electra* ready for its mission. Kelly Johnson was the reason the plant would be dubbed the "Skunk Works" many years later when its role in the development of the U-2 spy plane was discovered by Congress, but that is a story in itself.

Mantz would always feel guilty that he hadn't been able to prevent the crash at Honolulu and he never revealed what he knew about it. He married Terry Mac Minor on August 19, 1937. Mantz would die later after striking a hillock while skimming over the desert on a movie location. He would apply full throttle, but to no avail. The aircraft, built for the movie *Flight of the Phoenix*, would crash, killing him instantly. He would, just before his death, probably trying to ease his guilt about what had happened, tell Fred Goerner about what had been done to the *Electra* while it was being rebuilt at the "Skunk Works". Fred Goerner was a CBS investigative reporter who wrote the book, *The Search for Amelia Earhart.* The book was based on extensive research and contained numerous interviews with eyewitnesses to events surrounding the 1937 around the world events.

By noon of the 20th of March, all members of the crew of the *Electra* were booked aboard the ship USS *Malolo*. No one noticed Jim McNichol board just before they all arrived. He stood close to the gangway smoking a cigarette as Amelia and her party had boarded, followed by a small band of reporters. Chris and Mona had stopped to buy leis so everyone could throw them in the water when the ship left Hawaii, as was custom on the islands. Amelia gave a short press conference in her stateroom and thankfully they were only there a few minutes before the siren, signaling 30 minutes to departure, blew. None of them knew at the time that the *blown tire,* that crippled the *Electra* and ended what eventually became known as the first around the world attempt, would have tragic consequences for Earhart and Noonan.

Covers (envelopes) frequently autographed by Earhart were used as fund raisers to finance her expensive expeditions.

CHAPTER FOUR

MARCH 20, 1937

Luke Field on Ford Island, Pearl Harbor, Hawaii

The crippled *Electra* was carefully removed from its resting place on Luke Field's northeast/southwest runway. In spite of a steady tropical rain the depot maintenance crew removed the stricken aircraft to the depot hangar and secured it. Mr. Williams, an inspector from the Department of Commerce, arrived the next day and finished his investigation of the crash the following morning. Lt. Arnold made several drawings of the skid marks on the runway that could be positively identified as belonging to Earhart. The right tire marks were much wider than the left, which meant a blown tire was involved. Lt. Arnold had watched the crash in a state of horror. He had seen the left wheel leave the ground and had felt a little sick to his stomach when the right landing gear instantly snapped under the entire weight of the aircraft. In turn, the right wing hit the ground and the prop struck the runway stopping instantly. The screeching and thudding noises it made, as well as the sparks that flew, provided a show he would never forget. It haunted him. Arnold watched Mr. Williams inspect the aircraft, take fuel samples and make notes. While walking the runway, the inspector didn't pay any attention to the skid marks, nor ask any questions of any witnesses. On several occasions the young lieutenant had wanted to show Williams what he had discovered, but he had been given specific instructions by his superior, General Yount.

"We will give this Department of Commerce guy, what's his name?"

"Williams, Mr. Williams, sir."

"Give him all the assistance he requests, but do not and I say again, do not volunteer any information or present any opinions. This damn thing is a political hot potato and we don't need to get involved."

"Yes, Sir." Arnold didn't want to incur General Yount's wrath so he kept his mouth shut. That's the reason that the accident report never reflected that the tire blew before the left wheel came off the ground and disintegrated during the rest of the accidence sequence.

While preparing the aircraft for shipment Lt. Arnold had also inspected the props as they were pulled off the engines and found both of them in the low pitch or the correct take off position. He also inspected both valves on the left and right Oleo Struts and found that the valves and struts were in proper serviceable condition, precluding the failure of either strut. The right tire was so badly damaged from being dragged across the runway nothing could be learned from it.

Luckily for ONI there was no way anyone could tell what caused the tire to blow. Amelia felt that either the right Oleo Strut had failed or the tire blew on the right side. She leaned towards a blown tire. As usual, she was correct, but circumstances dictated that she would never know for sure.

The remains of the *Electra* NR16020 left Hawaii on the passenger ship S.S. *Lurline* on the 27th of March and arrived without incident at the Lockheed plant in Burbank, California on April 2nd. The *Electra* was to be fully rebuilt and made ready for a second attempt to fly around the world.

APRIL 4, 1937

Kelly Johnson's Office, Lockheed Aircraft Plant Burbank, California

The person in charge of the project, Kelly Johnson, left nothing to chance as the engines were immediately sent to the Pacific Automotive Shops for a thorough inspection and rigorous testing. Because Amelia had the presence of mind to shut both engines down immediately, there was minimal damage to the engines. The aircraft would, in the next two months, undergo a complete retrofit. The weak points in the fuselage that had surfaced during the crash sequence would be strengthened. Lockheed would make sure that everything was A-OK, as Americans like to say.

"Paul, we have to do what we can to convince Amelia that what the Man from ONI wants her to do is in everyone's best interest."

"I don't like it Kelly, not one goddamned bit. Everyone on board that aircraft could have been killed. It was by the grace of God there was no fire."

"Be that as it may, it's water under the bridge. I've got to play ball with this guy. Lockheed needs Navy contracts and this guy can stop them or make sure we get 'em. I don't have a choice; this company dies without Uncle Sam."

"He's got nothing I want though, nothing at all, I don't have to play ball."

Mantz sat down in one of the red leather chairs and poured himself a stiff drink from the decanter on the coffee table. Johnson sat down behind his massive, carved, black walnut desk just before Lanning arrived.

Mantz took a long sip of the 12 year old bourbon and sat back against the soft leather. "I'm here for Amelia, whatever she decides I will back her up. Personally, I hope she tells this guy from ONI to piss up a rope, although I don't think she knows how to do that. And if she decides to go along with whatever he wants, what then?"

"I will give her all the help I can and take everything I can get from ONI."

"You are a mercenary son-of-a-bitch aren't you?"

"Yes sir I am."

Lieutenant Commander Lanning arrived at precisely 2:00 as he had told Johnson he would. "Good afternoon gentleman."

"Good afternoon sir, Miss Earhart should be here at any moment."

Mantz simply held up his glass and nodded.

"We have a lot of work to do this afternoon; I want this wrapped up before I return home."

"Such as?" There was a slight surliness to Mantz's voice.

"Such as the aircraft. Mr. Johnson, how is it coming along?

"Very good, sir, I got your specs last week and everything is possible."

"Good, What about you Mr. Mantz."

"What about me, I didn't know I was supposed to do anything except provide the long distance flight instruction."

"I get the feeling, Mr. Mantz that you aren't exactly, shall we say enthused about this project."

"The truth is I'm not. I don't like your tactics and I don't think I like the fact that you're using one of my best friends for your own ends."

"Believe me; we wouldn't use her at all if there were another way."

Johnson's phone rang. He picked it up on the first ring; that's how nervous he was.

"Yes Violet……Send her in."

Amelia opened the massive oak door and was slightly taken aback. She didn't know Lanning and she hadn't expected Paul to be here. Although it was a little disconcerting, she recovered gracefully.

"Allow me," Lanning said, pulling out one of the heavy red leather easy chairs and nodding towards it.

"Thank you, although I must warn you I'm a little suspicious. All of you seem to be waiting for me and I don't know why."

"You will by the time you leave here today. Kelly, Mr. Mantz, shall we all be seated?" They sat down in the comfortable red leather chairs around the marble coffee table, all except Kelly, who stayed behind his desk.

"I will come directly to the point. The world situation is very precarious. Hitler has been making extraordinary territorial gains without firing a shot. Washington thinks it's just a matter of time before he starts shooting. It's the nature of the beast. Italy has already engaged in North Africa. They aren't very good at it, but they're still shooting. Japan is on the verge of invading China; we suspect that will happen very shortly. The Navy's concern is the Pacific and what the Japanese are doing there. We know that they are building military installations in the Japanese Mandated Islands, namely the Marshalls and the Marianas. We need proof of what they're doing, in short, we need pictures.

"And I suppose that's where I come in."

"Exactly Miss Earhart."

"It sounds like a big undertaking, one that would require a lot of training on my part. It also would require a great deal of planning. And, correct me if I'm wrong, it all has to be done in secret."

"You seem to have stated the mission in a nutshell. Kelly can give you the details later. What you must realize is the entire mission must be top secret. Not even your husband can be privy to the plans."

"That presents a problem; what about my navigator Fred Noonan, he must know exactly what is going on?" She mused, I'm not sure I like this set-up at all.

"We realize that and we don't have a problem with it. Mr. Mantz will give you all the training you need, both in long distance flying and aerial photography. Mr. Johnson will make all the modifications necessary to your airplane. Kelly, we have Clarence Williams on this one, he is a navy reserve Lieutenant Commander, and he'll do as he's told?"

"Good, he is the best flight planner around. Williams should do everything involving the flight, except the secret missions. Noonan will have to do that himself. I'm sure he is more than up to the task."

"Please tell me precisely what would my mission entail? Amelia queried a little nervously. She thought to herself, uh oh, what kind of mess are they trying to drag me into? I have a feeling they're going to try and squeeze me into a tight spot. God, it's hot in here. I shouldn't have worn this heavy shirt. No matter what, I will sweat in my socks. (This is a pilot's term for not showing fear under duress.)

"The primary mission is to photograph the Japanese installations on Truk Atoll in the Pacific. There are two secondary missions, which will be a good opportunity for you to get your feet wet with aerial photography, Miss Earhart. The first is the Burma Road all the way into China. The second is the west coast of Malay. That will be for the Brits; they will take the film from you in Singapore and reload your cameras."

She hesitated before she replied to give herself some time to digest what he had outlined and its possible ramifications. "I'm not that good with geography in that part of the world. Won't the flight into China require a lot of additional time; how will I explain that?"

"Headwinds are always a good excuse for being late. You will need to make a lot more speed when you are on a mission, but the *Electra* is more than capable of 60 mph over your usual 140 mph cruise."

"What do you have to say Kelly…Paul?"

"We can have the aircraft fitted with cameras by the end of the week. The *Electra* will require about another month to complete. We will start Clarence Williams planning the flight."

"Paul, where do you fit in?" Lanning glanced in Mantz's direction; the expression on his face was dead pan.

"I'll handle the training. We should be able the start with another *Electra* while yours is being repaired.

"Paul, I don't know that we can…" Lanning cut him off in mid-sentence.

"Kelly, surely we can find one, after all you do make airplanes here, don't you."

"We'll work something out, you won't want for an airplane."

Amelia couldn't wait to bolt. She could no longer contain her exhilaration. "If that's all gentlemen, I will go talk to Fred. You will have my answer by tomorrow morning." She could hardly wait to share the bombshell with Fred.

"Thank you for your time, Miss Earhart, I hope you decide in our favor."

"I've already decided sir; it's Fred that holds the key."

Lanning smiled and opened the door for her, there was nothing more to be said.

. . . .

Amelia drove her Cord up the Mulholland Drive hill to their North Hollywood home. She liked the mountain road's twists and turns and handled the fine machine like it was on a racecourse. She likened speeding in her Cord to flying. She could always think clearer when her adrenaline was flowing. When she got home she called Fred Noonan in New York and briefly told him about the meeting. She outlined the mission as best she could over the phone. "Well, Fred, what do you think, is it possible?"

"From a navigation point of view, most definitely; I

don't know the mechanics of it. Will we have the fuel for the extended legs of the trip? What do we know about aerial photography?"

"Off hand, I don't know. According to Kelly Johnson we have the fuel for a 4000 mile trip or maybe that just smoke and mirrors to get Perdue University to buy the airplane? George seems to think we have several really big benefactors, but they are always anonymous. The bill for the repairs to the *Electra* is going to be astronomical. It will probably take all the money we put aside for the round the world flight just to pay for fixing the aircraft after the Hawaii fiasco. I don't know if we have the money for another attempt. This gentleman could make it possible for us to make history."

"You don't have to sell me, Amelia. Remember what I told you after the crash in Hawaii?"

"Yes I do, Fred. You said, 'when you're ready to fly again, I'll be ready to go along.'Can we do it?"

"I think we can do just about anything, Miss Amelia Earhart, 'Lady Lindy', just about anything." This nickname became popular because she gained about the same fame as the world-renowned Charles Lindberg, who also reveled in breaking near impossible flying records.

"What about Mary, will she be all right with this?"

"She wants what I want and she can't know anything about what we're actually doing."

"George will be in the same boat. Seems a shame we can't tell them."

"Maybe not, they would probably just worry more. And, they'd probably just try to talk us out of it."

"Good bye Fred, I'm really glad you're going."

"Me too, Good bye."

Amelia felt good about Fred's attitude. He wouldn't go with her if he didn't think they could accomplish the mission. Tomorrow she would agree to the Man from ONI's mission. She heard the front door open, Ah, George must be home early. He has been doing that more and more lately.

"I'm home, Amelia."

"How are you this fine evening Mr. Putnam?"

"Just fine, thank you, Mrs. Putnam."

"I've been thinking George, Do you think the government is behind any of our benefactors."

"What makes you think that, dear?" A shadow crossed his face momentarily.

"Well, it's the depression, money is tight, and yet we don't seem to have a lot of trouble raising money for my flying."

"*You* don't have any trouble raising money. I told you when we were married that I would make sure you could do the things you wanted to do with respect to aviation. It's very expensive, but we've managed so far, haven't we?"

"Yes darling, you have managed very nicely, I have never wanted for gas money."

When Amelia arrived at Kelly Johnson's office a little after one in the afternoon the next day, she found Lanning, Johnson and Mantz waiting for her expectantly. They seemed on edge; very interested in hearing what she had to say. Here were three, high-powered professionals in their own fields, waiting for a woman to give them the go ahead to proceed. That didn't happen very often in the early part of the 20th century. Lanning was pacing and contemplating how a *no* answer could sabotage ONI's very best chance to get a real jump on the Japs. Kelly Johnson needed a *yes* to keep the company he worked for on a profitable course. Paul Mantz wanted a *no*, because he didn't trust the Man for ONI; there was something about him that didn't sit well with Mantz. Many years of experience guided his instincts that Amelia and Fred were being misled, but there was no proof. Anyway, the decision was not his to make.

"Gentlemen, Fred and I accept the mission. Be advised that there is a lot to do before we attempt this flight," Amelia announced confidently. No one noticed that Paul's shoulders slumped and he scowled at her decision.

"Don't worry, Miss Earhart, we will make sure that you get all the support that you need. These films are extremely important and we've got only one chance to get them. It must be done perfectly the first time." Smiling broadly for the first time, Lanning was extraordinarily relieved that Amelia had consented to the mission. "I will get with you after the meeting and we will go over what you need to read."

"Good! Paul, Kelly, we need my *Electra* as soon as possible. I would rather do the photo runs with my own aircraft. That way I will know exactly what I'm doing and what I'm doing it with." Amelia was enthused.

Kelly affirmed, "I understand, I will put a rush on it."

"Can you think of anything else that we need to discuss?"

"No Mr…It would sure help if I knew your name."

"Mr. Smith will do nicely or the Man from ONI."

"Mr. Smith it will have to be. Good-bye, Mr. Smith and have a good trip back to Washington," she said as she extended her hand for a firm handshake.

"Thank you, Miss Earhart, I'm sure I will"

After Lanning had left, Paul ushered Amelia out into the hall. "Are you sure you want to do this? I wouldn't trust this guy as far as I can throw him."

"I have to trust him. Like most folks, I don't understand all that's going on with the Japanese. I'm sorry to say I haven't paid much attention, but I hope that people in Washington know what they are up to. The government came to Fred and me for help; if we can help I think we should."

"Okay, as long as you watch out. It sounds to me like they haven't told you everything and this government character is holding a lot back."

"We are both sure; if we weren't, we wouldn't go. We have time to make a good plan and prepare for the trip. Besides the airplane is the best around for this sort of thing. Between you and Kelly I feel certain that everything will work out so Fred and I can finish what we started."

"I hope so." Paul certainly wasn't convinced, but he didn't want to cast a shadow on Amelia's dream. He would give it his best effort.

· · · · · · · · · · · · · · · · · · ·

Over the next five weeks Amelia, Fred and Paul Mantz spent countless hours going over every detail of the missions, especially the secret ones. Fuel was figured down to the last quarter gallon. Fuel burn was checked at all the altitudes and the airspeeds that they would use. Locations were selected where a mission could be aborted if things weren't just right. An alternate plan was developed if they couldn't locate either the Truk Atoll or Howland Island. The Man from ONI had advised her to fly every leg exactly as she was expected to do. She should maintain 140 to 150 mph and apply full power only on take-offs. When it was time to make the planned deviations from her publicly known course, the *Electra* would be flown at a fast cruise speed of 190 mph. Any differences that couldn't be made up with increased speed would be explained away by *headwinds*.

Amelia and Paul Mantz flew all over northern and southern California in a borrowed *Electra*, photograph-ing everything imaginable. They would deliver the film to the Kodak processing lab when they finished in the evening and pick up the photos the next morning. She learned how to make photo runs using the same cameras that were being installed in her plane. Paul spent many hours training Amelia to master specific flying and aerial photography techniques. Mantz mar-veled at how fast Amelia could absorb and retain these new ideas.

Amelia's *Flying Laboratory,* as she affectionately dubbed it, emerged from the Lockheed facility on May 19. It had morphed into a unique plane: there was no other *Electra* on the planet with its special features. A long focal length aerial camera had been secreted away under Noonan's desk in the back seat. It was perfectly camouflaged; it actually looked like part of his desk/map table. Also, there were two high quality cameras mounted in the wings. There would only be one opportunity to get the all-important aerial shots of Truk Atoll, so they used one German-engineered Leica Reporter 35 mm camera in each wing. The cameras were ingeniously hidden behind electrically oper- ated doors. The doors opened automatically when the camera was activated by a switch under the pilot's seat.

To say the customized *Electra* was Spartan was an understatement: they removed all the sound- proofing and the trailing wire antenna. Even the steel knobs were replaced with aluminum ones. Everything that wasn't essential was stripped from the plane. The belly antenna was re-positioned to allow for the installation of the camera under Noonan's map table. All these changes were to make up for the added weight of the cameras and film.

. . . .

The Man from ONI had also suggested they take off from Burbank without any fanfare. His intelligence agents had reported that there were Japanese spy rings operating somewhere near the Mexican border, so he felt it best to keep them as off balance as possible. To this end he had planted several rumors: Amelia was aborting her around the world attempt and hinted that it would be next year before she could try again.

The day after she accepted her retro-fitted plane and rolled it out of the Lockheed plant, Amelia, her husband George Putnam, and Fred Noonan boarded for a flight to Oakland, California. Her mechanic "Bo" McKneely, whom she called her good luck charm out of fondness and respect, pulled the wheel chocks and scrambled aboard. The flight to Oakland was to pick up some covers, which were their only cargo. On every record breaking flight she had previously made, she carried covers (envelopes that she autographed and sold). She stopped at a number of post offices along the way and mailed them to people who had gladly paid for the souvenirs. After all, these were from the famed female aviator that had been postmarked in exotic places. This was her husband's idea to help defray the high cost of her trips (gas, food, spare parts, repairs, etc.) Today those covers are coveted by collectors and are worth a great deal of money.

"It feels great to fly her again, doesn't it George?" There wouldn't be much conversation on the flight to Miami. It was close to impossible to hear very much because there was no soundproofing left. Fred had developed a simple communication method to compensate for this problem: he would pass a note from the back seat to Amelia, who was seated in the front, on the end of a slotted bamboo stick. She would scribble a reply and place it on the stick for Fred to retrieve while she was busy in the cockpit.

"If you say so, dear." George had his mind on money matters as he did most of the time.

They left Oakland the next morning, the covers safe in her attaché case. They arrived in Miami three days later, their jumping off place for the second attempt to fly around the world. They stayed in Miami for a week so Pan American mechanics could prepare the aircraft for the arduous flight ahead. The night before leaving Miami she and George were enjoying a quiet meal in the hotel dining room.

"Amelia, are you sure about this whole thing?" He always gave her a chance to back out of any endeavor gracefully.

"Very sure, George, Noonan is probably the best

navigator in the world. Did you see what he did on the over water portion of our flight here? We had seen nothing but ocean since leaving New Orleans. Three hours of nothing but water and he passes me a note telling me we would sight Tampa at 10 past noon; I laughed out loud, remember?"

"Yes I do. I was at a loss until you showed me the note and I had to laugh too. I wasn't laughing when we sighted Tampa a minute earlier than his estimate. I don't know how he did it, but I'm glad he did."

"That's why I say to you, don't worry, this is my last long distance flight and I think it will be the one I'm most remembered for. It's never been done before: around the world at the equator, 29,000 miles, the longest route possible."

"It has never even been attempted before, by anyone. You forgot to say *especially by a woman*."

"That shouldn't be a consideration, man or woman. We're all people and people are capable of anything."

"We should copyright that."

"Don't bother, I doubt anyone would want to use it."

"I tend to disagree."

"That is the beauty of our relationship, we can agree to disagree."

JUNE 1, 1937

5:56 a.m.
Miami Municipal Airport

The two Pan Am mechanics, John Cavendish and Ricky Shelton, who had spent the previous week working on the *Electra,* stood watching her take off roll. John was the first to speak after she broke ground. "There goes one hell of a lady."

"Damn right. I sure had the wrong idea about her when she got here. I thought she was just another woman pilot out on a stunt flight to get her name in the papers."

"We all did, Ricky, but she knows what she's doin'. She sure wasn't bitchy or uppity neither. She knew exactly what she wanted, but was always nice, very reasonable and damn, she had the patience of Job. Not hard to look at, too."

"True, I remember the second or third day she was here, I was looking for someone to hold some fuel lines out of my way while I looked at the turbocharger an' boom, she was there and held 'em for me. Imagine, did you ever have a pilot do that?"

"Not likely Ricky, most of them wouldn't get their hands dirty on a bet. You could have knocked me over with a feather when she showed up at lunch over at Mike's across the street. We're the only ones that eat there. I figured she would always eat at her fancy hotel. Not her, she must have eaten lunch at Mike's four or five times. And, she would sit down at the counter, just like regular people."

"Yeah John, I did some of my best work on that aircraft. I kinda feel like I'm up there with her, I sure wouldn't mind it. She's really something."

Their reaction to the dynamic, but humble persona Amelia had was typical. Whether it was a formal or casual setting, she left a trail of ardent fans from all walks of life.

Earhart and Noonan, now lone voyagers, lifted off from Miami Airport into the silver gray dawn of another beautiful Florida day. They were headed for Oakland California, but unlike other travelers they were taking the long way around going starting from the west and traveling east. Oakland to Miami was the first leg of the second around world attempt. This time there was no fanfare or publicity, no crowds or brass bands. And, she remembered her conversation with George: the right front seat was always empty on take offs and landings. Maybe the seat really was occupied in spirit, after all. *Rosie the Riveter*, the W.A.S.P.'s (Woman's Air Service Pilots) and the millions of women who would come out of their roles as homemakers to make the United States the war production capital of the world were all there. Rosie's spirit would be a bright light in the dark days that lay before both Amelia and the country. The winds of WWII were blowing. No one knew what was in store for Amelia and Fred, but for now the aviation gods were smiling on the *Electra* and its occupants as they left the shores of the United States for foreign points east.

The Burma Road
China
ndia
Kunming
Ruili
Jie Gao
Lashio
Vietnam
Burma
Laos
Bay of Bengal
Gulf of Tonkin
Rangoon
Thailand

CHAPTER FIVE

JUNE 1, 1937

Zona Norte, Tijuana, Mexico

The Zona Norte is a notorious section of Tijuana, Mexico. It was noted for its numerous bars and brothels, places that catered to pleasure-seeking soldiers and sailors from southern California. The Molino Roja was a well know brothel run by Mitsuru Yoshida. He prided himself on both his well-developed body and success since he emigrated from Japan in 1932. He had seen the possibilities of a well-run brothel in this section of Tijuana and had made Molino Roja one of the favorite spots with American sailors and marines stationed at the U.S. Destroyer Base at San Diego. American service men have a tendency to loosen up after a couple of beers, especially while enjoying the affections of a pretty young lady. Yoshida had "bugged" each room 1937 style. A system of tubes was run to each room and all of them ended up in his office. He always sat in his office during business hours and listened intently for any scrap of usable information. He heard everything that went on; and most importantly everything that was said. He wasn't just the operator of successful whorehouse, he was also was Imperial Japanese Navy Lieutenant Commander in the infamous Tokkeital (Japanese Naval Secret Police). His job was to keep track of American Navy ships entering and leaving the base and if possible, where they were headed.

He was enjoying a cup of coffee on the terrace before taking a shower. He had just finished his daily workout and was taking his time about starting his day. Suddenly, his houseboy burst onto the terrace and announced, "Yoshidasan, Amelia Earhart took off this morning to fly around the world."

"Thank you, Saburo, now get back to your duties."

"I thought you would like to know Yoshidasan. She took off from Miami at 5:56 this morning, headed for San Juan, I believe."

"Again Saburo, your duties!"

"Yes, Yoshidasan." He retreated from the terrace and went back to polishing silverware, but his ears were glued to the radio that was blaring in the next room.

It had taken all of Yoshida's self-control to contain himself over the news. He had been assured by the Kempeitai (Japanese Army Secret Police) that Earhart would cancel her attempt or at least postpone it until September or October, long after their invasion of China. He immediately alerted his assistant, Sato Fukushima, a 30-ish Japanese Naval Lieutenant who seemed to like nothing more than doing Yoshida's bidding. He was, for all practical purposes, Yoshida's right hand man.

"Get a message to Tokkeitai Headquarters immediately! Tell them Earhart has begun another around the world attempt. She left Miami at zero five fifty six this morning, heading east. Also, see if you can get that new girl?"

"Maria Helena?"

"Yes, she seems to be quite popular with Commander Jacobi from San Diego. See if she can get him to talk more about the due date for the Lexington Group. We need to keep track of their carriers."

"Yes sir! Will there be anything else."

"No, get that message sent!"

Fukushima virtually ran to the radio room. Yoshida went back to his coffee, but not as relaxed as he had been before the interruption.

JUNE 1, 1937

Office of Naval Intelligence
Washington, DC

Commander Lanning had been at his desk since 6:30 this morning. He wanted to see who was most interested in Amelia's takeoff. His vigilance paid off just after 11:00 o'clock.

"Morning, Yeoman Giles, is the old man in?" Giles nodded her head without looking up from her typing to see who it was.

"Thanks." Petty Officer Richard Connelly knocked on Commander Lanning's door; he had just come from the message room.

"Don't mention it," she looked up and smiled at him, he smiled back

"Enter!" Lanning commanded

Connelly stepped inside the austere office. Lanning was standing, looking at a map on the wall with his back to the door.

"We intercepted a message from the whore monger in Tijuana. Here's the raw copy. The translation should follow in about 45 minutes. They sent it in the Red code. We've been reading that one for months.

"Thanks Connelly, I'll put the translation in my records, there is an advantage to being fluent in Japanese, especially in this job."

"Aye, Aye sir, will there be anything else?"

"Giles will have a message to be sent in a few minutes."

"Very good, sir."

Connelly left as Lanning began to read the message. A smile crossed his face as he finished reading. Good, he thought, that ought to give the bastards at Tokkeitai Headquarters something to chew on. He knew that the Japanese Secret Police hated surprises and this one came out of left field.

"Giles, come in here I need to send a message." Giles, his Petty Officer Yeoman, was used to these requests. She immediately presented herself in his office, steno book in hand. The meaning of the message wasn't readily apparent to her, as was the case with so many of the Lieutenant Commander's messages.

TOP SECRET

EYES ONLY: ASSISTANT CHIEF
BUREAU OF NAVIGATION
OPERATION COVEY WATCH IS NOW

OPERATIONAL. SURVEILLANCE ON
COVEY'S ROUTE AND ASSOCIATED
SHIP MOVEMENTS NEEDS TO
COMMENCE AS SOON AS POSSIBLE,
PER THE OPERATIONS PLAN. MOLINO
ROJA INFORMED HIS HQ OF COVEY'S
DEPATURE THIS a.m. AS WE SURMISED.
STANDING BY.
SIGNED L

He received the following reply an hour later:

OPERATION COVEY WATCH MESSAGE
RECEIVED ALL NOTIFICATIONS MADE.
SIGNED N.

JUNE I, 1937

Tokkeitai Headquarters,
Saipan, Mariana Islands

The officers in charge of Tokkeitai Headquarters
on Saipan were not accustomed to being taken by

surprise and Amelia's take-off from Miami caught them flat-footed. Orders were immediately sent to Tokkeitai Headquarters at Kwajalein Atoll. The orders were to cover Amelia Earhart's entire route of flight and monitor her operations from "fishing boats" and anything else that would float. The Tokkeitai was very paranoid about any American activity in the Pacific. Their philosophy was to prepare for every contingency. They worried about the possibility of an over-flight of one of their secret installations in the Marshalls or, even worse, their base at Truk Atoll. If she flew too close to their territory, the Japanese military felt they were ready to deal with the incursion. They would find out that they were sadly mistaken in their assumption.

The Japanese Imperial Navy deployed the "fishing boats" all along Earhart's proposed route of flight. Their mission was to track her progress and note any deviations from her planned route. They also prepositioned three seaplane tenders, all capable of taking an aircraft such as the *Electra* aboard and transporting it to Kwajalein. The Major General in Charge of the Tokkeitai Headquarters at Kwajalein felt the sting of scrutiny by his superiors, who were watching from their relatively safe perch on Saipan. He gave orders that her transmitting frequency was to be monitored around the clock. The Japanese Navy had a network of low frequency Direction Finding stations throughout their possessions in the Pacific. They were set to get a radio fix on her aircraft if she transmitted on 500 Kilocycles. He surmised that she would fly in the opposite direction of her first attempted flight. This, thanks to the press, was well publicized. The orders from Saipan were quite specific, all communications mentioning the matter were to be transported by courier and *not* broadcast over the airways. They relented on their order and allowed normal radio traffic to dispatch the seaplane tenders and "fishing boats".

His orders were, "If she does invade Japanese territory, she must be forced down by whatever means available and transported to Saipan via Kwajalein." The entire incident was not to be discussed over the radio and above all, no notification was to be given to the Kempeitai (Japanese Army Secret Police) head-quartered at Taihoku, Formosa. The entire effort to intercept Amelia, if she overflew Japanese territory was to be a secret Imperial Navy Operation and would not go beyond the navy's lines of communication.

The increased activity was all being duly noted, logged and transmitted to ONI via the high frequency direction finder tracking stations operated by Pan American Airways on Hawaii, Midway, Guam and Wake Islands in the Pacific. These stations, completely unknown to the Japanese, had been tracking ship movements in the Marshalls and the Northern Pacific by intercepting their High Frequency Radio Transmissions. This clandestine activity had been going on for several years. There were only six High Frequency Direction Finders in existence. Hawaii, Midway, Guam and Wake Islands each had one, as well as Los Angles, California. The sixth one was, as of that date, being prepared for deployment to Howland Island to aid Amelia in finding Howland Island.

JUNE 6 – 18, 1937

Around the World Flight Continues

The around the world flight's route was generally along the equator. From Miami, she hopped to Puerto Rico, then to east coast of South America. The route took them down the coast from Venezuela to Dutch Guiana (present day Suriname). She continued her flight to Brazil and then, finally, to Natal, Brazil on the eastern-most tip of South America. During the flight she wrote in her journal while the autopilot allowed her a few minutes of respite. She met, analyzed and solved the problems, both in the air and on the ground that arose during this once-in-a lifetime undertaking. She felt that the flight would help women gain acceptance in the field of aviation and other areas previously closed to women.

At 3:15 on the morning June 6th they took off from Natal bound for Dakar, French West Africa, the entire route that day was over the Atlantic Ocean. At 4:27 p.m. that same day they landed at St. Louis, Senegal, sadly not their intended destination. When they had reached the coast of Africa, Noonan had given Amelia course correction to the south to arrive at Dakar, French West Africa. She had overridden that advice, as was her prerogative, and made a northerly correction. This decision brought them to St. Louis, Senegal near dusk so they spent the night rather than attempt the flight to Dakar in darkness. Even in the 21st century the pilot-in-command of any aircraft is given the latitude to accept or ignore anyone if he or she thinks it isn't in the best interest and safety of the aircraft, passengers or the mission. As with all aspects of human endeavor, someone can be wrong and the sign of a good leader is one who accepts responsibility, admits their mistake and moves on. She stated in her journal that she chose to ignore his advice and felt she was right. She never, to anyone's knowledge, did the same thing again. The next day they made the relatively short trip to Dakar, French West Africa on Cape Verde, the western most point on the African continent. This concluded the portion of their journey that followed established air routes of the day. The next portion of their trip would take them over terrain that few traveled, especially the scheduled air carriers.

The next 7 days were spent skipping across the African continent. From Dakar across French Equatorial Africa, Goa, French Sudan and Khartoum they flew to Assab on the southern end of the Red Sea. They stayed the night in preparation for their hop over the Arabian Peninsula to Karachi, India (present day Pakistan). This was part was quite politically and religiously sensitive, because the sands of Arabia were sacred and the Arabs feared an emergency that would force her to violate the sacred Arabian sands. Early on the morning of the 15th they took off on their trip to Karachi. The flight ended that afternoon without incident, much to the relief of the Government of Arabia. Violation of the sacred sands of the Arabian Desert was bad enough, but by a woman was unthinkable.

Amelia and Fred began their trek across the sub-continent on the 17th, after a rigorous inspection of the engines by the Pratt and Whitney mechanics.

They took off for Calcutta, India in Bengal Province via Allahabad, India. The plane touched down at Dum-Dum Airfield just after four in the afternoon. She was a little concerned about the monsoons, which were supposed to begin in mid-June. The locals told her that the season could start at any time. The winds shifted to the southwest during this season, meaning their course would put the winds right off their nose. As she noted in her journal, "……no flyer welcomes rains of the density of Indian downpours, especially when there are sudden mountains to slap against and squashy fields to bog down in." The landing fields were all sod strips and attempting a take-off with an overloaded aircraft in a rain-soaked field is no easy feat. At dawn on the 18th the Electra took off from Dum Dum field into the gray dawn bound for Rangoon, Burma. "The plane clung for what seemed like ages to the heavy sticky soil before the wheels finally lifted and we cleared with nothing at all to spare the fringe of trees at the airdrome's edge," was her description of perhaps the most precarious take off of the trip to date. In addition to the stress of the take-off, their anxiety was increased by having to fly the route dictated by ONI and detailed by Paul Mantz, not their publicly announced route.

Amelia climbed her plane to 8000 feet and pushed the throttles forward to 200 miles per hour indicated airspeed (232 miles per hour true airspeed) and headed straight for Myitkyina in Northeastern Burma. Click, click, click, she made a photographic run on the Burma Road that passed near the airfield, and then continued her east-northeast course. The nimble *Electra* easily climbed to 10,000 feet on her way to Xiaguan, China and another portion of the Burma Road. The increased altitude boosted her true airspeed to 240 mph, essential to keep on her schedule. From Xiaguan, China she flew and photographed the Road into Burma. Noonan, too, was taking pictures from his specially equipped navigator's table as the flight progressed. Amelia was using the switch under her seat to activate the wing cameras.

They touched down at Akyab, Burma at 11:51 that morning. She simply mentioned to the airport authorities that she had left Calcutta at 7:00 o'clock. The airport authorities assumed she meant 7:00 a.m. Calcutta Time. This left the impression that the flight had taken 4 hours and 51 minutes, when it had actually had taken an hour longer, evidenced by her taking on 400 gallons of fuel instead of the projected 200. She wrote in her notes that: "Much of the way from Calcutta to Akyab we flew very low over end-less rice patties. Some waved hats, others turned back to their work. Their every mood reflected in a shining flood." No one would suspect from reading her journal what she was really doing. She checked the weather and took off bound for Rangoon, Burma at approximately 1 o'clock.

Shortly after takeoff they were hit by a monsoon rain which she described as "an unbroken wall of water which would have drowned us if our cockpit hadn't been secure. After trying to get through for a couple of hours we gave up, forced to retreat to Akyab." They flew out to sea to avoid the mountains because visibility was only a "few hundred yards". She wrote in her notes "By uncanny powers, Fred Noonan managed to navigate us back to the airport, without being able to see anything but the waves beneath our plane." "Two hours and six minutes of going nowhere" was Fred Noonan's capsule view of the endeavor.

"Do you think the weather will improve tomorrow?"

"The airport manager simply smiled shook his head and said, "Sorry, Miss Earhart, when the monsoons begin, they last for three months. Every day it's the same weather, sorry."

She felt quite lucky that she had gotten the pictures of the Burma Road in China when she did Her deviation had been a practice run for the mission in the Pacific two weeks later. That one would require a much larger deviation from their intended course. But this one had neither hostile air forces to contend with, nor hostile armies waiting for their arrival. The route had been over land with many airports within reach if they had run short on fuel or had some unforeseen mechanical problem.

Amelia and Fred never knew that the photographs they had taken would be used for terrain maps of Northern Burma and China: maps that would be critical during World War II. "Vinegar" Joe Stilwell, Commander of U.S. Forces, would build the Ledo Road, an American lifeline to Chang-Kai-Shek's beleaguered Nationalist Chinese Army. Orde Wingate's "Chindits" was a British Special Force made up of British, Burmese and Indian Gurkha soldiers. Merrill's Marauders, a deep penetration special operations unit, would conduct long range attacks into Japanese territory in an attempt to disrupt the Japanese supply lines and rear areas. The British Army would open ground supply routes to Chang-Kai-Shek's Nationalist Army by forcing the Japanese out of Burma. The first half of this mission would be the least known of her accomplishments and the most productive in terms of aid to the Allied war effort many years later. The second half of her mission wouldn't be as helpful to the British later on. In fact, the opposite would be true.

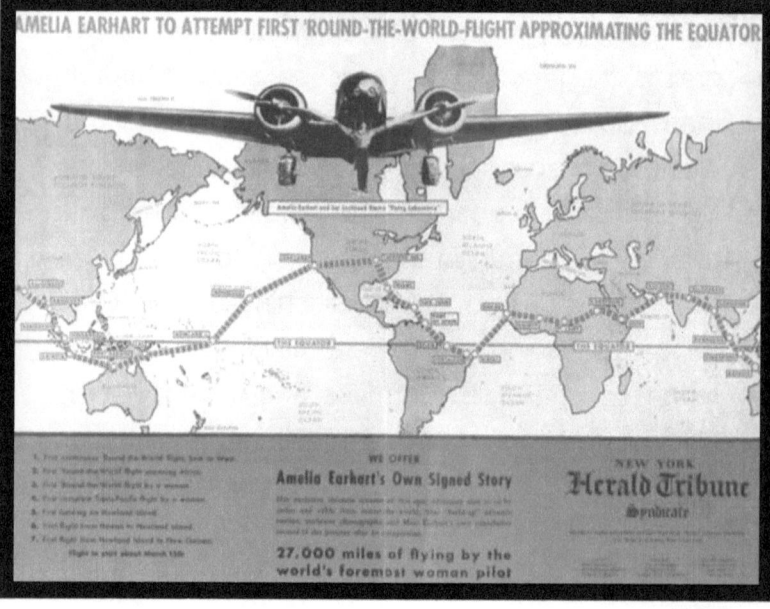

CHAPTER
SIX

JUNE 19, 1937

Akyab, Burma

Amelia decided that today wasn't going to be a replay of yesterday even though the weather was the same, maybe worse. She attempted to fly low under the torrential tropical rainclouds. It was literally coming down in sheets. She couldn't see more than a quarter of a mile ahead even though she was flying as slow as she could and still keep the *Electra* airborne. After 20 minutes of extremely dangerous low level, slow flight she decided to trade extremely treacherous flying conditions for just treacherous. She eased the throttles forward and pulled back on the control yoke to try and fly above the mountains. In a few minutes she leveled off at 8000 feet: high enough to clear all the mountains around but not high enough to get out of the clouds. For the next 2 hours she literally flew blind in the clouds until she was certain they had cleared the mountain range that separated Akyab from Rangoon. The stress of the flight made them both tired and they decided not to go on to Siam (present day Thailand). They stayed in Rangoon and enjoyed the sights on the road to Mandalay.

The next day took them to Bangkok, Siam, the "Venice of the Orient," so named because the streets were canals at one time. But the canals had been drained long ago, then filled and roads put in their place. Sadly, this caused the city to lose some of its charm. They landed at the Bangkok airport, one of the best they had encountered so far on the trip. After refueling and checking the weather reports, it was off on the nine hundred mile journey to Singapore and the completion of the mission they had begun on the Burma Road to the north.

This leg of the flight didn't require any deviations from their planned route. She wrote about her trip across the Gulf of Siam to the Malay States in her journal. "I felt as if I were dreaming, to be flying over such fabulous waters, with the shores of Siam on the right and Cambodia on the left. As we wound southward along the eastern coast of Malay and then across the peninsula to Alor Star there looked up from the charts stretched out on my knees marvelous names like Bang Taphang, Lem Tanne, Koh Phratnog (today's Paradise Island). The sea, really mauve, melted into a blue sky with companies of little white clouds marching through it. A fairer day could not have been. The monsoon and its perversities were well behind us."

"I thought there was no more weather like this."

Typical male practicality, she thought.

The trip along the western coast of Malay wasn't just for the sake of avoiding the storms in the mountains to the east. It was to photograph specific locations and terrain along this coast for the purpose of making maps and planning fortifications. She made a number of photo runs, both for the photos and practice for their future mission. By the time they reached Singapore they had covered the entire west coast of Malay. She landed at the new nine million dollar airport, "an aviation miracle of the east," according to Amelia. The city was a marvel, less than 100 years old and it was the tenth busiest seaport city in the world. It was the crossroads for trade linking Europe, Africa, India, Australia, China and Japan.

. . . .

While Amelia and Fred slept at the home of the American Consul General, Monett B. Davis and his wife, the *Electra* was undergoing some "unscheduled maintenance". At about one o'clock in the morning two men picked the lock on the hangar door. One of the men was Donald Jamison from the British Embassy Passport Control Office, a cover for MI-6 agents operating out of the British Embassy. Jamison had been a long time agent of MI-6 and work like this was quite routine for him. The other man was Major Robert MacMasters from the Intelligence section of Sir William Dobbie's staff. Dobbie was the General Officer Commanding Malaya.

Jamison opened the lock on the hangar door with a set of lock picks that he always kept in his pocket. MacMasters closed and locked the door from the inside as Jamison made his way across the hangar floor guided by the shielded beam of his flashlight.

"Do you think anyone will see the torch, Donnie me boy?"

"Doubtful, my good man, doubtful."

"You hold the torch and I'll get the film out of the fuselage camera."

"Okay"

"Damn, the cabin door is locked, you're up, Donnie."

Jamison made quick work of the lock on the rear door of the *Electra* and within 20 minutes the film canister was out of Noonan's under-the-table camera and MacMasters was just finishing replacing the exposed canister with an unexposed one.

"Robert, get down, someone's coming." The shop foreman was checking the hangars before leaving for home. He tried the door and seeing it was locked he went on to the next hangar.

"Whew, close one Donnie."

"It's not really close unless the bugger taps you on the shoulder and asks what the hell you are doing. Now that's a close call!" MacMasters knew Donnie well enough to know what he had described must have happened to him at least once. It seemed that Jamison had no nerves left; that nothing fazed him.

"I'll take the left wing camera and you…"

"Get the right, yes, yes I know." By 2:15 a.m. the large magazine from under Noonan's table and the two small ones from the two Leica Reporter wing cameras were on the hangar floor. Donnie was finishing locking the back door on the plane.

"We got all three magazines?"

"Yes, Donnie, they are right there on the damned floor!"

"Easy, old boy, all three cameras are loaded with fresh film to answer your next question." Donnie smiled at MacMaster's agitation.

"Then we're ready to leave?"

"Yes, Robert, we're ready to leave." Donnie took the knapsack off his back, packed all three magazines inside and slung it over his left shoulder. MacMasters unlocked the door and the both went outside.

"Hold the light while I relock the door."

"Will do, can you hurry this up a bit?"

"It's done." Both men walked to the fence that bordered the south side of the airport. MacMasters retrieved the blanket he had left there and threw it over the barbed wire on the top. They climbed the fence and walked to their jeep. The entire operation had taken an hour and forty three minutes, two minutes less than Jamison had planned.

General Dobbie's staff was headed by Chief of Staff Brigadier General Arthur Percival. He was the man, who on February 15th 1942, would surrender Singapore to the Japanese in what Winston Churchill would term "the worst disaster and largest capitulation in British history." But, in 1937 Percival was drawing up a tactical assessment of how the Japanese invasion of Malay would develop. Percival was greatly handicapped in his assessment, because London hadn't sent the aircraft that they had promised. He was very dependent on photographs provided to him from "other" sources. Amelia and Fred has just become an invaluable resource.

In April of 1941, when Percival was made General Officer Commanding Malaya, he had no way of knowing that the tactical assessment he had written back in 1937 had been handed to the Japanese, including maps produced from the aerial photographs made by Amelia Earhart! The Japanese received the assessment not via espionage or such skullduggery, but through military channels. When the Germans rolled over France in May of 1940, part of the instrument of surrender was the partitioning of France into the German Occupied Zone and the "Free Zone" administered by Vichy France. Vichy France was a German puppet government. In September of 1940 Vichy granted Japan access to the Tonkin region of French Indochina (presently Vietnam), which greatly aided Japan to further put pressure on Chang-Kai-shek's Army during the Second Sino-Japanese War. The Vichy also handed over many secret documents from their military liaisons with Britain and other Allied countries. Had the British not sent their Gibraltar based Force H Fleet to destroy the French Fleet at the battle of Mers-el-Kebir and the battle of Dakar in 1940 , then one of the most modern battle fleets in the world surly would have fallen into the hands of the German Kriegsmarine (Navy). Sadly, this action resulted in the deaths of almost 1300 French sailors. The Vichy French Government was neither neutral, nor secretly allied with Britain or any other allied power. The Vichy not only gave up, but they switched sides. The end result of this bit of treason was the resounding defeat and humiliation of the British Army in Malaya, greatly facilitated by the political maneuvering of Vichy France, Hitler's Germany, Japan and Siam. But, all this was in the future. Presently, all Amelia and Fred knew was that they had accomplished the first mission for ONI; the most difficult one lay ahead. They lifted off the runway at Singapore at dawn the next morning of June 20.

They arrived in Darwin, Australia on June 27th. The *Electra* had undergone a full servicing and safety of flight inspection at Bandung, Java. They had encountered the first maintenance problems of the trip, but these had been taken care of by the capable mechanics of K.N.I.L.N (a sister company of K.L.M. Airlines). Amelia had two things she wanted to accomplish in Australia. The first was to contact Jean Batten, Australia's famous woman pilot. Jean was in Sydney at the time, however, she did send Amelia a telegram wishing her the best of luck. Seeing a koala bear was also on her list of things to do in Australia, but this also didn't happen. The direction finder radio had malfunctioned on the hop between Timor, Dutch East Indies and Darwin.

She spent both days in Australia getting the radio repaired and ridding the aircraft of as many items as they dared. They removed their parachutes and anything they felt wouldn't be needed and shipped it all back to the states. Amelia decided to finish lightening the aircraft at Lea, New Guinea and that included emptying her suitcase almost in its entirety. The only luggage she kept intact was her attaché case, containing all her official paperwork and passports. Weight was a very real concern for the trip across the Pacific. She even begrudged the six pound wooden stick that was used to that was used to measure the amount of fuel in the inboard tanks. She was even heard to lament, "That's an extra gallon of fuel." More weight, more fuel burned, it's a simple fact of life. Weight was such a huge factor that they were very, very focused on getting it done correctly; after all, their lives depended on it.

The *Electra* gracefully lifted off the airport at Darwin at dawn on June 30th headed for Lea, New Guiana. All along their route they had been extra careful not to exceed 150-155 mph. It was essential that this pattern was followed to the letter. Paul Mantz had made this extremely clear during her training.

"Your ETA's (estimated time of arrivals) must always be consistent with an indicated airspeed between 150 to 155 mph, even on the legs that are secret and off the published course line. If they aren't someone will become suspicious and then the secret missions won't be secret anymore." Mantz had never missed an opportunity to make this point.

The 1200 mile trip to Lae, New Guiana took 7 hours and 43 minutes and was without incident. Amelia turned the plane over to the very capable mechanics of Guinea Airways, Limited. They scru-tinized every aspect from stem to stern. The work was personally supervised by Amelia, as well as the airline Chief Engineer, Mr. Finn. The process was efficiently completed by the morning of July 1st. It included fitting the starboard (right) engine exhaust with a new cartridge for the Cambridge Exhaust Gas Analyzer (a very necessary instrument for long dis-tance flying because it allowed her to lean the fuel mixture to obtain the minimum fuel consumption under all conditions).

But poor weather, adverse winds and the inability of Fred Noonan to get a valid time signal caused them to scrub the planned midday departure on July 1st. A time signal was necessary for Noonan to check the accuracy of his chronometer. Knowing the time to the second was of critical importance for his navigation. Each second the chronometers are off results in a one mile deviation from the true position. AN ERROR OF FIVE MILES COULD MEAN THE DIFFERENCE IN FINDING OR NOT FINDING THE ISLAND. HE DID NOT KNOW IT, BUT THE PRINTED LATITUDE AND LONGITUDE POSITION FOR HOWLAND ISLAND WAS APPROXIMATELY FIVE MILES OFF ON ALL AVAILABLE 1937 CHARTS.

She received one of the two weather reports she requested that day. The report from the island nation of Nauru read as follows:

"THE FOLLOWING FROM NARAU STOP NEW NARAU FIXED LIGHT LAT 0.32 S LONG 16.55 EAST 5000 CANDLE POWER 5600 FEET ABOVE SEA LEVEL VISABLE FROM SHIPS TO NAKED EYE AT 34 MILES STOP ALSO THERE WILL BE BRIGHT LIGHTING ALL NIGHT ON ISLAND FROM PHOSPHATE FIELD WORKINGS STOP WEATHER 8 AM BARO. 29.908 THERM 84 WING (wind) SE

3 FINE BUT CLOUDY SEA SMOOTH TO
MODERATE STOP PLEASE ADVISE TIME
DEPARTURE AND ANY INFORMATION RE
RADIO TRANSMISSIONS WITH TIMES".

This message was very important because
Nauru is near the halfway point of the publicized
route. Nauru is of far more importance than a mere
checkpoint on a straight route. IT WAS THE KEY
NAVIGATIONAL AID THAT NOONAN NEEDED TO
KEEP THEM ON COURSE AND ON TIME. The lack
of a weather report from Rabaul was disheartening
and was one of the reasons she hesitated to take
off on the first. Rabaul was to the north of the publicized course line. She needed to know all she could
about the weather conditions to the north, but that
was not to be.

At 6:35 a.m. that morning Amelia had performed
a 30-minute test flight of the *Electra*. All was satisfac-
tory except she was unable to get a null on her DF
radio. A null was necessary to tell when the plane's
antenna was directly in line with the station. This
told the pilot that they were somewhere along a line
that bisected the sending station. The problem with
this form of Direction Finding was the pilot couldn't
tell their position along the line (how many miles they

were from their destination). She told Finn, "I think the station is too powerful and I was too close to get a null."

The plane was then filled with 87 Octane Aviation Fuel. One tank, containing 100 Octane fuel specifically used for takeoff, wasn't "topped off" since no 100 Octane fuel was available at Lae. The powerful flying machine stood ready on the very edge of the vast Pacific Ocean with 1100 gallons of fuel, oil tanks full and stripped of all unnecessary weight. Noonan finally got a good time signal from Adelaide station at 10:20 p.m. that night and noted that his chronometer was three seconds slow. He got another time signal from Saigon at eight the next morning, which confirmed the chronometer's accuracy from the signal the night before.

"What do you think about the take-off time, Fred?"

"We need to take off at 10:00 o'clock if we are to be at Truk by three this afternoon."

"Three should be good, because the light will be behind us and it will show the shadows. My understanding is that photo interrupters need shadows to judge building heights. Mantz said three in the afternoon was ideal."

"Then ten it is"

That would put them at Howland Island at seven

thirty in morning. It would give them enough time to get some sleep before taking off for Hawaii. After 19 hours in the air they would really need some sleep.

All was set, at 9:45 A.M the starboard (right) Pratt and Whitney S3H1 radial engine's 600 horses roared to life, and three minutes later the port (left) engine followed suit. At 9:51 a.m. the Lockheed Electra NR16020 taxied into take-off position at the north-west end of the 3000 foot runway.

After the engines reached operating temperature Amelia smoothly pushed the throttles forward, released the brakes and the overloaded *Electra* lumbered down the grass strip. With approximately 300 feet to spare the plane broke ground. Four hundred feet further it descended below the cliff at the end of the runway, momentarily out of sight of the spectators, mostly Guinea Airways Pilots, holding their collective breath. She didn't hear the loud praise delivered by the Guinea Airways pilots for an excellent takeoff as she descended to 5 or 6 feet above the water to stay in ground effect and eased the throttles back. As a careful, experienced pilot, she always observed the one minute limit at full takeoff power. With a slow climb, so slow that it was only 100 feet above the momentarily calm waters of the Solomon Sea, the plane just seemed to disappear into the haze. From the moment the crowd lost sight of it, they became a mystery. A mystery that 75 years later people still get excited about.

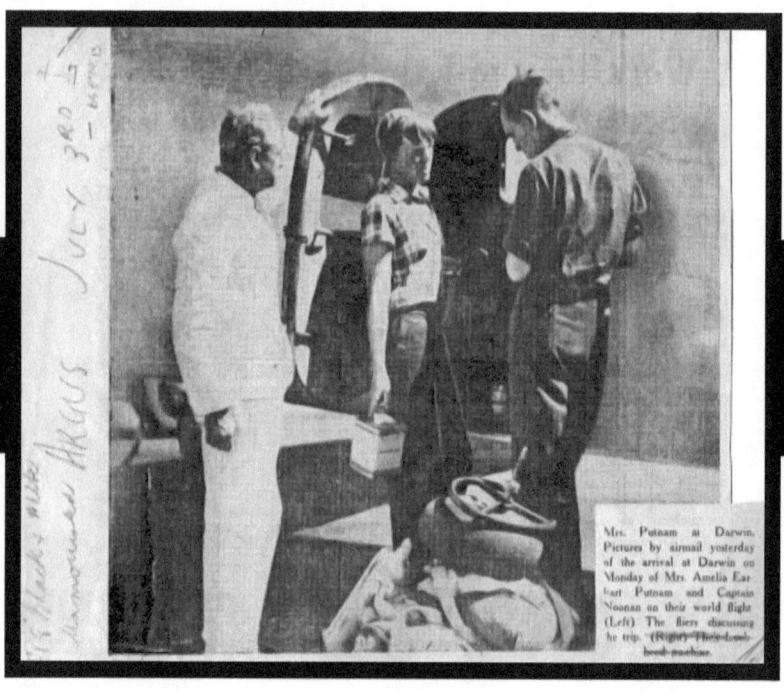

Amelia and Fred leaving survival gear in Darwin, Austrailia.

CHAPTER SEVEN

JULY 1, 1937

They climbed at 130 mph to 5000 feet over the Solomon Sea before making a left turn just past the coastal town of Bua. It would look to anyone watching that she was turning north to intercept her publicized course line which ran west to east near the inland town of Bokasu. She took up a heading of 021 degrees as Noonan had advised. With her usual smooth touch she leveled off at 10,000 feet as they left the north coast of New Guinea. Noonan passed her a note and she gave him thumbs up after reading it.

> 38 MILES TO UMBOI ISLAND, LAST
> LANDFALL FOR A WHILE. LOOKS LIKE
> WE HAVE A SLIGHT TAIL WIND. WILL
> KNOW EXACTLY WHEN WE GET THERE.
> HOLD 021 DEGREES.

Twelve minutes later they crossed the coast of

Umboi Island, 40 miles north of New Guinea, and Noonan confirmed their ground speed of 188 mph. The winds were 110 degrees at 29 mph just as Lae Radio had reported in the message sent shortly after Amelia's takeoff. Noonan was quite busy now. There were no checkpoints along their route until their destination, which they must hit "right on the money" the first time. Noonan had designated it on his charts as Point A. It was in the middle of the vast, seemingly endless Pacific Ocean 998 miles north north-east of Lae and 80 miles west of Truk Atoll. Noonan would need all his navigational tricks to identify this point as he would have no valid checkpoints except Umboi Island. That small, isolated piece of land was only 44 minutes into the 5 hour and 30 minute flight. After Unboli, until they reached their destination at Howland, there would be nothing to look at except the sun, the moon, the stars, clouds and water. She was to give position reports at 18 minutes past every hour. Amelia, Lanning and Mantz had decided to keep position reporting to a minimum to avoid detection by the Japanese. They had agreed that three reports were best. The first would be given four hours into the flight at 2:18 p.m. Lae time. "HEIGHT 7000 feet, SPEED 140 KNOTS, 695 MILES FROM LAE, EVERYTHING OKAY", she said. As luck would have it Lae Radio received all the transmission except the "695 MILES FROM". Because these transmissions were meant to lull the Japanese into a false sense of security, it was good if they were somewhat vague.

The second transmission was very important because it was more than just part of the ruse. It was a signal to Station Baker, the ONI listening post on Guam, alerting them that they had reached Point A and were preparing for their photo run at Truk Atoll. It was to be made a minute later than the other calls and the text was very important. "HEIGHT 10,000 FEET, POSITION 150.7 EAST 7.3 SOUTH, CUMULUS CLOUDS EVERYTHING OKAY" It was bewildering to the people at Lae; and, contrary to its intended purpose made the Japanese suspicious. ONI had decided on the exact wording of the report. The report was their actual position except the 7.3 NORTH had been changed to 7.3 SOUTH. This was very confusing to everyone listening because it placed them 257 miles east south-east of Lae and 84 miles south of their publicized course. After five hours of flying they should have been 750 miles northeast of Lae. The question on everyone's mind was: Is she on her way back to Lae?

The Japanese suspected something was amiss, but they didn't know what. None of their prepositioned "fishing boats" had spotted the *Electra* since the boat stationed in the Solomon Sea six miles off the coast of Lae had reported her takeoff. But, there was always a possibility of her flying past the posted boats unseen due to the local rain squalls that were reported in the area 300 miles east of Lae. Earhart's plane could have been obscured by cumulus clouds. The buzz on Kwajalein and Saipan increased markedly because the call made no sense to the Japanese. At times things that made no sense to one person usually made perfect sense to someone else. It was the old adage: "Take the obvious and reverse it." In this case the obvious isn't obvious; just like common sense isn't quite as common as we would like to think.

JULY 2, 1937

ONI Headquarters, Washington, D.C.

The position report was received loud and clear by Station Baker on Guam and flashed immediately to Station Item at Imperial Beach, California. It was finally relayed to Station US at Navy Headquarters (now the

Naval Security Command at Ft. Meade, Maryland),
also the site of the National Security Agency (NSA).

The Japanese Red code was also hot. Messages were flying thick and fast between Saipan
and Kwajalein.

Then the message arrived; just what the Man
from ONI had been awaiting!

FLASH   FLASH   FLASH

UNIDENTIFIED AIRCRAFT OVER
TRUK ATOLL REPEAT UNIDENTIFIED
AIRCRAFT OVER TRUK ATOLL,
ESTIMATED ALTITUDE 10000 FEET
SPEED APPROXIMATELY 175 KNOTS
MAKING ZIG ZAG PATTERN. PURSUIT
AIRCRAFT HAVE BEEN LAUNCHED.
REPEAT PURSUIT AIRCRAFT HAVE BEEN
LAUNCHED. PLEASE ADVISE FURTHER
COURSE OF ACTION

A worried look danced across his face; he knew
the chances of Japanese aircraft catching the *Electra*
were fifty/fifty. He would be almost as tense as Amelia
and Fred for the next two hours. He wouldn't relax
until he was sure they had reached a point where

the Japanese would have to turn back because of lack of fuel. He failed to realize that the orders from the Japanese navy had been quite explicit. "She is to be brought down at all costs." This meant that the loss of one or more aircraft from fuel exhaustion was deemed an acceptable loss. So, if there was a chance that the fighters could find her, they were to remain aloft until they ran out of gas, period.

"Giles, come in here I need to send a message!" he yelled, forgetting the intercom on his desk in the heat of the moment. The message again made no sense to Giles, but she took it down and made sure it was sent with all due haste.

TOP SECRET

**EYES ONLY: ASSISTANT CHIEF
BUREAU OF NAVIGATION**
COVEY HAS FLOWN OVER THE CROWS
NEST AND IS HEADED HOME. WILL
ADVISE IN TWO HOURS OF STATUS.
SIGNED L

The Assistant Chief of the Bureau of Navigation simply smiled when he read the message and put it aside. So far so good, he thought to himself and with quiet authority he continued the meeting with the Chief of the Air Navigation division. He was a bespectacled Lieutenant Commander by the name of Weems.

. . . .

Noonan had fixed Point A by using a radio signal from the Pan American navigational beacon on Guam and another one on Wake Island. He knew he was located exactly where the signals crossed. From Point A, Amelia turned the plane eastward towards Truk. She had purposely delayed her take-off to 10:00 a.m. so that they would arrive at Truk around three in the afternoon. The sun would be behind them in the western sky at a good angle to cast the necessary shadows for the best photo results. She made a zigzagged single pass over the Atoll taking pictures at a furious rate of anything that looked like an installation: harbors, airfield, gun emplacements and so on. They had spent only 34 minutes covering the 95 miles between Point A and Noonan's second turning point. Upon arrival at Noonan's Point B, she turned east-southeast and kept the needle on the airspeed indicator at 159 mph.

While she maneuvered to establish them on their

new course, Noonan, using the wooden measuring stick, "stuck" the custom long-range internal fuel tanks. After adding the readings from the cockpit's fuel gauges he wrote her a note.

"It looks like we have a little over 740 gallons of fuel remaining. Traveled 1100 miles and used approx 370 gallons. 1294 miles to original course line, then 1065 miles to Howland. We should reach original course at 1030 GMT."

She was still apprehensive; the Japanese had launched one aircraft that she had seen. Neither of them was sure of its type or capabilities. Noonan had seen another fighter at the fueling point at Truk and he wasn't sure if it had also been launched. They still had 2359 miles left to go. The *Electra* was making a ground speed of 170 mph or just less than three miles a minute. If those refueling aircraft were A5M's, forerunner of the A6M Zero of WWII fame, they would be doomed. The A5M could climb at just under 2800 feet per minute and had a maximum speed of 273 mph. Hopefully, their turn to the east-southeast instead of taking a direct course to Howland would fool any pursuers. She was out of sight of anyone on Truk when she made the turn. The fighters didn't have on-board radar. Also, according to intelligence reports, the radar at Truk wasn't fully operational yet, so her chances were excellent. That is, of course, if the intelligence reports were correct. The Man from ONI had warned the pair that the Japanese would have aircraft aloft over each one of their island possessions looking for them. Fred Noonan's job was to make sure that they didn't get close to any other Japanese held islands.

Both Amelia and Fred were locked in private contemplation and remained tense for the next 2 hours. They half expected a Japanese fighter to appear out of nowhere, then it would be all over. The *Electra* was a sitting duck: too slow to outrun a fighter, not nimble enough to out maneuver it and was unarmed. One good reason for the lack of effective pursuit on behalf of the Japanese Naval Air Force was that almost all of the front line aircraft were staging far to the west for the invasion of China, scheduled to begin on the 9th of July. Only three aircraft were still stationed at Truk. All three of these aircraft were capable of intercepting the relatively slow-moving *Electra*. However, two had just finished a routine security patrol and were refueling when she over flew the secret installations. The third one was in one of the new maintenance hangars.

One of the fighter pilots, Navy Lieutenant Takahashi, chose to get airborne immediately. The other pilot, Navy Lieutenant Goto, finished refueling. As a major, Goto would one day in the future lead the Japanese squadrons that bombed Pearl Harbor. Lieutenant Takahashi didn't find her because he guessed, wrongly, that she would head directly to Howland Island on a heading of 100 degrees for 2200 miles, the shortest distance and most logical choice. When he reached the point at which she had turned east-southeast, he continued on a 100 degree heading intending to pass north of the British owned Gilbert Islands and south of the Japanese Mandated Marshall Islands. Thirty minutes went by without sighting Earhart. He then turned back towards his home base with low fuel problems of his own and made it back to Truk with very little fuel to spare. The second aircraft was about a half hour behind her, but he also took up a 100 degree heading and flew to the Marshall Islands just barely making it on his fuel. Goto didn't see the elusive *Electra* either. Many hours later one of the ever watchful Japanese "fishing boats" spotted the *Electra* southeast of Nauru Island on its publicized course line. Only then would the Japanese Navy realize that she had turned south-southeast to intercept her publicized course.

At precisely 7:18 p.m. Amelia made another pre-arranged, coded radio call that would make several people at ONI and at least two people in the White House breathe a collective sigh of relief:

"POSITION 4.33 SOUTH 159.7 EAST HEIGHT 8000 FEET OVER CUMULUS CLOUDS WIND 23 KNOTS."

This was another cryptic message telling the White House and ONI, who were continually monitoring the mission, that all was well. Amelia had evaded the Japanese and they were well on their way to intercept their publicized route. The mission seemed a success but no cheer went up in either location or on board the *Electra*. The proof would be in the photographs that were taken of Truk and that could only happen if she made it to Howland Island.

As Paul Mantz and Kelly Johnson had predicted, she had to periodically reduce the throttles to maintain 159 mph. This was because fuel was being burned off making the aircraft lighter. Less weight meant that less power was needed to maintain the same speed. Using less power leads to burning less fuel; less fuel burned leads to more miles per gallon. These axioms are facts of life in the world of aviation.

It was 1015 Greenwich Mean Time (GMT), 10 hours and 15 minutes after takeoff, and they were nearing the intersection of their publicized route at Point C, as Noonan had dubbed it.

"How far to our publicized course line?" She screamed this over the drone of the engines after spotting what she thought were the lights of a ship ahead.

"About 80 miles." He yelled back.

On an impulse, even though it wasn't her assigned talk time, she felt compelled to speak and give something of a position report. "Ship sighted ahead" This jewel from Amelia was so much more than a casual observation. It would eventually establish her whereabouts at a precise time. James Johnson was third mate on the SS *Myrtle Bank*, which was approximately 100 miles south of its intended destination of Nauru. It was on a voyage from New Zealand. He heard an aircraft off the starboard quarter that night. The radio operator at Nauru transmitted information on Amelia's call at 1030 GMT after he had tried in vain to contact the Lockheed to get more information. The call would be logged at 1030 GMT and over the years it has been assumed that time is when she actually had made the call. But, she had really made the call at 1017 GMT. The radio operator on Nauru broadcasted a report of the incident to Bolinas Radio at 1031 GMT after trying in vain to get her to respond to his return calls.

The *Electra* turned onto its publicized course at 1037 GMT, 7 minutes behind Noonan's estimate. Thirty-two minutes later a Japanese "fishing boat" radioed Kwajalein with the news that the Earhart flight was at 2 degrees 19 minutes 55 seconds south and

169 degrees 12 minutes and 54 seconds east, slightly more than 4 miles south of her publicized course at 1109 GMT. Long ago the Japanese had learned how to make sure everyone was using the same point of reference for time. This was quite necessary due to the vast wilderness of the Pacific Ocean, as well as the great distances that separated their mandates. GMT (Greenwich Mean Time) was the easiest and most efficient way to make sure everyone was on the same clock. England, Germany and many other countries, as well as American and many foreign merchant ships used the GMT system. This was something the American Navy hadn't learned yet. Their insistence on using local time would result in confusion in the future. The *Itasca's* use of local time would foster problems that would quickly become insurmountable. At precisely 0948 GMT the aviation gods stopped smiling on the two American voyagers. The luck that had been with them thus far was beginning to run out, slowly, steadily and without regard for future consequences. Amelia and Fred were in trouble and they didn't know it yet.

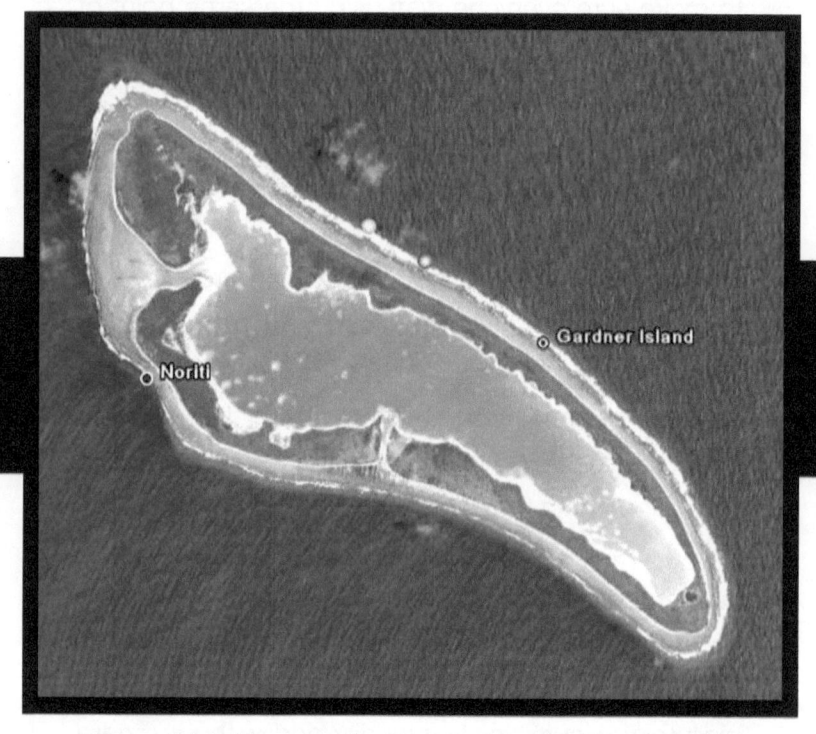

Gardner Island (present day Nikumaroro, Republic of Kiribati).

CHAPTER EIGHT

JULY 1, 1937

Nauru Island, Central Pacific Ocean

There is an old saying in this business: "Aviation is not inherently dangerous, but like the sea, it is very unforgiving of mistakes." Very seldom does an accident just happen. Sometimes an accident sequence begins when the pilot gets out of bed in the morning or maybe with an argument with a spouse weeks prior. Or, it could be a shortcut taken by a mechanic months before.

For every accident there are always clues, a progression of mistakes and missteps that lead the talented investigator to the final scene of the calamity. The case of Fred and Amelia is no exception. At 0948 GMT Fred Noonan did a sighting on the navigational light at Nauru Island. He had planned their course to pass within 34 miles of the island for two reasons:

> #1 They couldn't afford to take the chance that anyone on Nauru would spot them as they were still 174 miles northwest of their

publicized course. This was too much to explain away as a navigation error.

#2 The navigational light was visible to ships at 34 miles according to the telegram they received at Lae. Noonan wanted to make sure they were able to see the light no matter what their altitude.

Unlike a sighting on land, at night on the open ocean there are no visual cues to orient the observer as to distance away from any light or object. Celestial navigation is the only way to figure the distance away from any given feature. If the observer uses a sextant correctly, the process is normally very accurate.

Finding your position on the face of the earth is not terribly involved, but it requires the utmost care. The sextant is calibrated for the surface of the ocean because all readings are taken in degrees above the horizon. If the navigator's sighting was higher than sea-level the reading on the sextant will not be accurate and therefore his calculations will not be accurate. All sightings, taken from an aircraft must be corrected for altitude; this was quite a problem in World War II. Bomber navigators had to use celestial navigation to find their targets because of the lack of detailed charts. A great many bomber missions dropped their bombs an average of 5 miles off target. It is simple to see why: the navigators that didn't correct for their altitude above the ground or their chronometers were as little as 5 seconds off. Most missions were dropped from 25,000 feet (almost 5 miles high). If the sightings weren't corrected for altitude the drop would be 5 miles off! Five seconds on the chronometers would also result in a 5 mile error! The loss of Amelia Earhart began with the addition of an extra zero by the individual who typed the message that they had received on June 30th while they were still at Lae. (It should have read 560 feet, not 5600 feet!)

THE FOLLOWING FROM NARAU STOP
NEW NARAU FIXED LIGHT LAT 0.32 S
LONG 16.55 EAST 5000 CANDLEPOWER
5600 FEET ABOVE SEA LEVEL VISABLE
FROM SHIPS TO NAKED EYE AT 34
MILES STOP................................

The sighting that Noonan took caused him the plot their position incorrectly. Because of this, his wind speed and wind direction calculations were wrong. In other words, all his calculations from then on were wrong because of the mistake at Nauru. The course correction that Noonan gave Amelia steered her south of course. For every mile she flew towards her destination she also was steadily going further south of course. This wouldn't have been a huge problem in the daylight because 508 miles east north-east of Point C is Tabiteuea Island. This is an excellent checkpoint as it is easily recognized: it is a submerged reef that is 41 miles long with small islands above water. The publicized course line that Noonan had plotted passed just off the north end of the island, but because she was steadily drifting south they actually flew over the southern end, about 40 miles south of course. Two other factors added to their problems on that fateful night on July 1, 1937. There was a waning crescent moon resting 45 degrees above the horizon that provided limited illumination and a layer of clouds partially obscuring their view.

"That should be Tabiteuea Island down there!" He exclaimed this as he climbed forward over the fuel tanks to sit in the cockpit.

"If you say so, Fred. Aren't we supposed to pass of the north side of the island?"

"Yes, I would say that those breakers out your side are on the north side of the island. Noonan was pointing towards some white water breaking on a reef.

"How far does that put us off course?"

"About 3 miles. Actually not bad for 500 miles

without a star sighting. Just hold your course and we should arrive about six to ten miles south of Howland. That way when we get there you can turn north-northwest and the rising sun won't be in your eyes.

"Very considerate of you Fred."

Now, throw a modern term into the mix: human factors. When Noonan made the initial mistake, he had been awake for 18 an hour stretch, about 10 hours in the *Electra*. Flying then wasn't the same as it is today. It was incredibly noisy. It had no temperature control, meaning it was exceedingly hot or cold depending on the altitude. Also, there was little or no air circulation, so gasoline fumes would have been present. In order to make her ETA's (estimated time of arrivals), she had to fly at 10,000 feet. So now throw in oxygen deprivation: maybe not enough to be especially dangerous, but definitely enough to make someone feel more tired and fuzzy-headed than at sea level. By the time the tired pair arrived at Tabiteuea Island, they had been up for almost 24 hours, about 16 and a half hours in the plane. Most likely Noonan and Earhart saw an island that looked somewhat like they anticipated it would and thought they were right on course. Their exhausted brains would have easily accepted this thought because they wouldn't have to do any extra work.

No Japanese "fishing boats" spotted her after

the initial one near point C because she was drifting steadily south of course. No chatter on the Red code was of concern to the Man from ONI because he had welcomed the Japanese keeping track of her progress. These messages provided the only way for him to know her exact location in the vast Pacific.

Noonan did some final fuel calculations. "We've got a little over 200 gallons of fuel remaining in the wing tanks. The tanks in the cabin are empty."

"That's almost five and a half hours of flight time. How far do we have to go?"

"According to my figures we've got 225 miles to Howland."

"That means we'll have...about 3 hours of flight time left, if anything goes wrong.

She smiled at him; it was her idea of a joke. She had full confidence in him.

JULY 2, 1937

Early Morning100 miles from Howland Island

Amelia was forced to end her musings of the past

and was shocked suddenly into the reality of the present day by a nudge of the bamboo "note stick."

TURN LEFT TO 335 DEGREES, I THINK WE ARE SOUTHEAST OF THE ISLAND.

There we go again with I think. I would be much happier with I know. She would never let Fred know she had any doubts about his navigational skills. She kept those thoughts to herself. What the hell could have happened? Fred is the best navigator in the world. I've seen his work for a month; he is phenomenal! What's going on?

"Can you see Howland yet?" He yelled over the constant drone of the engines.

"I can't tell, the clouds are casting shadows on the water and the shadows all look like islands."

"What? I can't hear you."

"Never mind!" she shouted waving her hand "I'm getting under these few clouds so I can see better." Her words were lost in the cockpit. Noonan merely shrugged his shoulders. Amelia's hands went to the throttles and pulled them both back slightly and pointed the nose down. I'll level off under these clouds; looks like a thousand feet will do it.

As they descended she started some quick fuel calculations. It was 1900 GMT by her watch and she calculated she could spend about 40 minutes looking for Howland before she had to give up the search and begin executing her alternate plan.

Another note came forward. IT'S OUT IN FRONT OF US. I DON'T KNOW HOW FAR, I NEED TO MAKE ANOTHER SIGHTING.

She scribbled a note and put it in the slit at the end of the pole. SHOULDN'T WE BE CLOSE BY NOW?

YES WE SHOULD BUT I DON'T THINK WE ARE.

At 1912 GMT she tried to raise the *Itasca*. "KHAQQ CALLING *ITASCA*. MUST BE ON YOU BUT CANNOT SEE YOU. BUT GAS IS RUNNING LOW, ONLY A HALF HOUR LEFT, UNABLE TO REACH YOU BY RADIO, WE ARE FLYING AT 1000 FEET."

Glancing at her watch she thought, I've got to break this off and head for Gardner Island at...1935 GMT. I'll fly northwest 15 minutes and see what happens. The next 15 minutes were excruciating. Amelia continually searched the water ahead. Back and forth she scanned desperately looking for an island, black smoke, some sign of land or the *Itasca*. At 1926 she called the *Itasca* as a last ditch effort to make the rendezvous. "KHAQQ CALLING *ITASCA* WE ARE LISTENING BUT CANNOT HEAR YOU. GO AHEAD ON 7500 WITH A LONG COUNT EITHER NOW OR ON THE SCHEDULED TIME ON HALF HOUR." At this point the 19 and half hours into the flight and 26 plus hours without sleep were beginning to tell. Her voice sounded stressed and so was she. She had just told the *Itasca* to broadcast on 7500 Kilocycles so she could get a fix on them. Her Direction finder would only work up to 1500 KC. There was no way she could get a fix on the Coast Guard Cutter on that frequency. She heard the long count on 7500 and tried to pick it up on the wrong radio. This could happen to any pilot if they became as fatigued and over-wrought as Amelia had become on her long, long, journey.

At 1930 GMT she made another transmission that was received by the *Itasca*. "KHAQQ CALLING *ITASCA* WE RECEIVED YOUR SIGNAL BUT UNABLE TO GET A MINIMUM, PLEASE TAKE BEARING ON US AND ANSWER ON 3105 WITH VOICE".

At this point she did a 180-degree turn because they both knew that if they were northwest of Howland Island, flying northwest would place them further into the trackless ocean to the north. If she flew southeast, though, they might fly over Howland Island. In case they couldn't locate Howland she would switch to her alternate plan: fly to Gardner Island which was 400 mile southeast of Howland. They would ditch as close to the island as possible and swim to shore. In any event, it was 1942 GMT; they hadn't crossed Howland and the half hour she had allotted to find the tiny island had come and gone. 93 miles was the closest she had gotten to Howland. It was time for a clear-headed, coldly calculated decision, in many instances the kind that save lives. It was extremely difficult to cope with the discomfort of such a grueling trip: 20 hours of her body being in the same position, a lack of sufficient oxygen, non-stop deafening noise, noxious fumes and temperature fluctuation. This was not to mention the fatigue brought on by almost 27 hours without sleep and the current stress of not knowing their exact position in this barren, unfamiliar part of the world.

Her mind began to race. If I give up looking for Howland now, that's it, years of planning and hundreds of thousands of dollars flushed down the drain. If I don't go to Gardner and continue to search for Howland, I not only risk my life, but Fred's as well. That's not an option. It was different when I was alone, but now I'm responsible for someone else. Sorry, George. Sorry, Mr. President and ONI, but our lives are more important than this flight. Amelia made her decision and without further hesitation, she continued southwest towards Gardner.

She wrote a note to Fred. GIVE ME A GOOD HEADING TO GARDNER ISLAND. WE ARE ABORTING THE MISSION IF WE ARE NORTH OF HOWLAND AND SEE IT ON THE WAY WOULD BE GREAT BUT

I DON'T THINK OUR LUCK IS THAT GOOD. GET US TO GARDNER FRED, I KNOW YOU CAN.

Noonan wrote back, 337 DEGREES WE ARE DEFINITELY SOUTHEAST OF HOWLAND, CAN'T TELL HOW FAR YET.

At 2013 GMT she keyed the mic and made a call to the Itasca. "WE ARE ON A LINE OF POSITION 157/337 WILL REPEAT THE MESSAGE ON 6210 KILOCYCLES." She switched her radio to 6210 KC and repeated the message.

Her spirits ebbed as she climbed to 8000 feet and her normally nimble mind was becoming sluggish as she felt her adrenaline drain away. She started dwelling on her failure. What would the world think? I've failed to fly around the world, not once, but twice. Both failures occurred on the way to Howland Island, I wonder if that's fate, I believe we make our own, but that is a little too much of a coincidence. I wonder if anyone will donate for a third attempt. What will George think? What will he say? Her mind snapped back to business as she realized she hadn't told the *Itasca* what they were doing on the 157/337 line of position, at 2025 GMT, She keyed the mike and simply stated "WE ARE RUNNING NORTH TO SOUTH."

Fred pushed another note forward. TUNE YOUR DF RADIO TO TITUILIA RADIO BEACON. SEE IF

YOU GET A NULL ON THAT ONE, IT SHOULD START COMING IN SOON.

She gave him a thumbs-up and tuned the radio. Tutuila was on American Samoa at the navy refueling station. Later it would become Station Victor as part of the High Frequency Direction Finding Network that monitored Japanese ship movements in the Pacific.

Another note came forward. KEEP THE NEEDLE 6 DEGREES TO STARBOARD AFTER YOU GET A GOOD SIGNAL. Amelia again answered with a thumbs up. The aviation gods were still not smiling on the flight, but their only hope was that they weren't frowning yet.

JULY 2, 1937

Earlier the same morning
Tokkeitai Headquarters, Kwajalein Atoll

Lieutenant Commander Ohayashi was shocked at the transmission at 1912 GMT and excitedly ordered. "Go get Lieutenant Commander Sato…immediately"

The young private bolted for the door to the Intelligence Section and boldly stepped inside. "A knock is required when entering this area, Private." Sato kept his usual calm but firm attitude.

"Sorry sir." The young soldier turned to leave.

"Now that you're here what do you want?"

"Lieutenant Commander told me to come get you sir."

"Tell him I will be right there."

"Yes sir!" The young soldier turned on his heel and went back to the radio intercept room.

Sato walked into the radio room five minutes later and inquired, "What is so bloody important, Ohayashi?"

"It looks like the miracle might be happening."

"Speak clearly Ohayashi, What miracle?"

"Earhart is having trouble finding Howland Island."

"Surely, you're kidding."

It was at that moment that Amelia's 1930 GMT call to the *Itasca* came over the speaker. They both listened intently.

"You're right Ohayashi, she is in trouble. I doubt if her on-board radio has the ability to get a fix on such a high frequency.

"You're right! She seems to be stressed, listen to her voice."

"Maybe, just maybe, we got lucky." They both listened intently to every word coming over the speaker: both from Earhart and the *Itasca*. They were elated when her 2025 GMT call stated that she was running north to south. Sato swung into action. He contacted his commander and updated him on the situation. The captain of the *Kamoi* (a 1922 vintage Japanese seaplane tender, ironically built by the New York Shipbuilding Company) was put on alert for a possible mission. The *Kamoi* was 2 hours out of Kwajalein bound for Ise on the Japanese Home Islands. The captain was instructed to return to Kwajalein immediately to pick up priority cargo.

Sato requested to switch to the newest code (dubbed the Blue code by ONI) as soon as possible. He was concerned that the Americans might possibly have cracked the Red code. This mission was too important to allow even the slightest chance of detection.

At 2230 GMT, two hours after her last call to the *Itasca*, Amelia made her last call, which was monitored by only two stations, Nauru and the Tokkeitai on Kwajalein Island.

"LAND IN SIGHT AHEAD".

The transcript of the call got lost in a confused bureaucratic maze of messages between the Australian authorities and the U.S. State Department. The Japanese didn't have a similar problem. Within 30 minutes Sato and Ohayashi had narrowed her position to somewhere in the Phoenix Island group.

The Phoenix Group was a British-controlled group of islands about 400 miles south-southeast of Howland Island. Sato immediately notified his commander of her landing. As the message slogged it way through the bureaucratic morass in Australia bound for Washington D.C., the old Japanese seaplane tender, the *Kamoi*, had reversed course for Kwajalein at full speed.

JULY 2, 1937

Approximately 11:00 a.m.
Gardner Island, Phoenix Island Group
(present day Nikumaroro)

Both of their spirits lifted at the sight of Gardner Island, the first land they had actually seen since their over-flight of Truk Atoll. That seemed like ages ago. They both were confident that they would be picked up within two days because the Man from ONI knew her plan to fly to Gardner in the event she didn't locate Howland. Nothing could have been further from the truth. Secrecy again, as it so often does, raised its ugly head. Yes, only Mantz, Johnson and the Man from ONI knew her plan, but Mantz and Johnson had been assured that ONI would notify the Coast Guard Cutter *Itasca* if it became necessary. ONI hadn't seen fit to read Commander Thompson in on the plan as they felt he had no need to know until there was a problem. The alternate plan was a good one; ONI felt there would be plenty of time to act if a problem arose. As is so often the case, people have a tendency to underestimate the abilities and tenacity of their enemies; in this case the mistake was fatal.

Fred scratched his head as he looked at the only available depiction of Gardner Island: a chart dated 1872. (See image at beginning of chapter.)

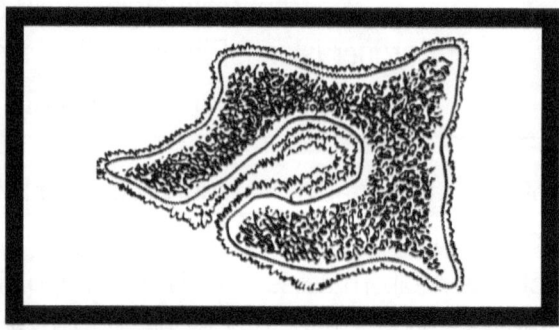

It looked no more than two miles in length and had an inlet on the west side of the island that almost cut the half mile island in half. The island they were looking at was easily four miles long and a mile and a half wide with a large lagoon in the middle. He peered through the windshield and said, "That's not Gardner, it must be an uncharted island in this chain."

"It's looks better than Gardner; I actually think I can land on that reef there on the southwest side."

"I will go back and get a position for this island so you can broadcast to the *Itasca*. I'm certain this isn't Gardner."

Her immediate thought focused on another problem. If they broadcasted their position as Gardner Island and the *Itasca* steamed to Gardner, they wouldn't find them! It would be best to give a latitude and longitude for this island and say it was uncharted.

At 2215 GMT Amelia made the call that would result in their rescue. "LANDING ON UNCHARTED, UNINHABITED ISLAND FOUR DEGREES FOUR ZERO MINUTES SOUTH, ONE HUNDRED SEVENTY FOUR DEGREES THIRTY TWO MINUTES WEST, 158.44 DEGREES FROM TUTUILA RADIO BEACON, WILL ATTEMPT LANDING"

Beside her in the cockpit again, Fred asked, "where are you going to land?"

Near that wrecked freighter on the west side of the island. I think the reef is the flattest there just to the north of ship."

Fred was somewhat distracted with last-minute calculations. He was sure that they were very close to Gardner, so close they should be able to see it. He was sure of his calculations, so the position of Gardner must be slightly off. The reported location of Howland was five miles different than its actual position: this inaccuracy was a common occurrence at that time.

Amelia turned the *Electra* on a five mile final approach. She cranked the flaps down to the "full flap" position and reduced power on the two Pratt and Whitney power plants. Her approach began by reducing the airspeed to just above the stall speed.

She told Noonan who was still busy with last minute calculations, "brace yourself for the landing, it may not be the smoothest one I've ever done." Noonan, still preoccupied, didn't follow Amelia's lead. He had not cinched his shoulder harness tightly. Amelia held her speed just above stall until she was about ten feet above the reef and then she cut power completely and let the plane sink till it hit the reef with teeth jarring force. This was the same technique used by carrier pilots to land in the shortest distance possible except carrier planes had landing gears that were built to absorb most of the shock: not the case with the *Electra*. She hoped the landing gear on her plane would withstand the impact. What she didn't foresee was Fred's failure to fasten his belt securely. On impact, the *Electra* bounced two feet into the air and settled back down with another jarring impact. Noonan's upper body flew forward. The left wheel fell into a hole in the coral after only 300 feet of ground run and stopped momentarily causing the aircraft to spin left. The force threw Noonan's head into the right side of the cockpit below the side window. They stopped on the coral reef about 150 feet off the beach in approximately six inches of water. She switched the magnetos off and for the first time in over twenty-one hours the engines were silent. The around the world flight was over. There was no way to fly their faithful chariot was going to fly off the reef. This was possibly its final resting place.

Amelia had been thrown about, but because her harness had been tight her injuries were relatively minor, but nonetheless painful. The harness had bruised two ribs when they were spun so violently. The sore ribs and many bruises were the extent of her injuries. Noonan, however, was quite a different story. He had a nasty head wound on the right side of his head, which she didn't have time to evaluate, and he was semi-conscious. She opened the hatch on the roof above her head, as quickly as her pain would allow, and heard only the sound of the surf breaking about 175 feet to her left. Her achy body complained as she crawled out of the hatch and down the wing and into the ankle deep water. Amelia opened the back door, rummaged around until she found a rag, dipped it into the water and made her way back to the cockpit to try to stop the bleeding from her partner's head wound. The trip up the wing was much more painful than the trip down. It was about half an hour before Noonan was conscious enough to crawl over the tanks and out the rear door. He leaned quite heavily on Amelia as they walked to the beach. Upon reaching dry land, both collapsed in the sand and lay there in the warm sun with only the sound of the surf breaking on the reef 200 yards away.

The most disconcerting fact was that neither of them knew exactly where they were. They still hoped help would come quickly. They had no inkling that the comedy of errors was going into its second act.

JULY 2, 1937

Afternoon of the same day
ONI Headquarters, Washington, D.C.

Lanning sat at his desk with an unbelieving look on his rugged face. The message he had just received was still in his hand. It simply read:

EARHART FAILED TO LAND AT
HOWLAND, WHEREABOUTS UNKNOWN,
WE ARE BOARDING THE *ITASCA* TO AID
IN SEARCH. PLEASE ADVISE.
CAPTAIN COOPER

Cooper and his party of three Noncommissioned Officers (NCO's) had been sent to Howland Island to supervise the repair of the runways on the island. After landing they were to remove all the cameras and film from the plane and service it for the flight to Honolulu. ONI didn't want any hint to leak out about the plane's real mission.

"Giles, come in here please."

Giles popped into his office, fresh from lunch with her boyfriend. "Yes sir?"

"Take a message."

A little after one fifteen Giles filed the following message.

TOP SECRET

**EYES ONLY: ASSISTANT CHIEF
BUREAU OF NAVIGATION**
COVEY DOWN PROBABLY AT
ALTERNATE. COAST GUARD HEADED

NORTHWEST NEED TO MOBILIZE
ASSET FROM PEARL. MONITORING
COMMO FROM KWAJALEIN
SIGNED L

Thirteen minutes later, the Assistant Chief of the Bureau of Navigation, Captain Chester A. Nimitz, notified Headquarters Pacific at Pearl Harbor that they needed to dispatch an aircraft carrier or capital ship to the Phoenix Islands to search for Earhart. The aircraft carrier USS *Lexington* wasn't ready to sail from San Diego, California yet. So, before 2 p.m. Washington, D.C. time the Chief of Naval Operations in the Pacific dispatched the battleship USS *Colorado* and its three seaplanes to search south of Howland Island to the Phoenix Islands for Amelia Earhart. The Captain of the U.S.S. *Colorado*, Captain W.L. Friedell, was to assume command of the entire search until further notice.

At 3:15 local D.C. time Lanning received the following reply:

TOP SECRET

ALL EGGS ARE IN THE *COLORADO*'S
BASKET, USE CAUTION WHEN
COMMUNICATING WITH OUR ASSETS,

DON'T GIVE AWAY ANY OF OUR
INVOLVEMENT UNLESS ABSOLUTELY
NECESSARY, CHIEF NAVAL OPERATIONS
PACIFIC WAS TOLD TO SEARCH THE
PHOENIX ISLANDS, THAT SHOULD SUFFICE
SIGNED N

JULY 3, 1937

Between 1:00 and 1:30 a.m.
Waters off Howland Island

14 hours after Amelia landed on Gardner Island a Japanese "fishing boat" approached Howland Island from the east and two "fishermen" paddled to the southeast shore in a rubber boat. A shadowy figure walked to the southwestern beach away from the airfield. He flashed three long, one short and two long dashes with his flashlight. Two men disguised as fishermen rowed to the beach in the boat's dingy. The three men spoke at great length and then the two "fishermen" returned to their boat. By 2:45 a.m. they had encoded a message and sent it in the old Red code.

FLASH

ITASCA HEADED NORTHWEST
TO SEARCH, ISLAND ALMOST
DESERTED. ADVISE
MARU ITO

They were answered at 4:23 a.m., by Tokkeitai HQ Kwajalein:

MARU ITO
CONTINUE SURVEILLANCE,
REPORT ANY MOVEMENTS
TOKKEITAI HQ KWAJALEIN

Tokkeitai Headquarters received permission to begin using the Blue code at 6:42 on the morning of July 3rd, a little more than 19 hours after Amelia landed on Gardner Island.

At 3 p.m. that same day Japanese Imperial Naval Captain Kozaka, Captain of the Japanese seaplane tender, *Kamoi*, boarded his ship, He had just received a face to face briefing from his commander who had been updated an hour before by the chief of the Tokkeitai on Kwajalein. His orders were to steam with all possible speed to the position Amelia had given, which was in the Phoenix Island Group, near Gardner Island. Kozaka had been handed a set of sealed orders to be opened only after he arrived at the island. He also was ordered to maintain total radio silence, except as directed by the sealed orders, until he reached the Marshall Islands on his return trip. He gave orders and within 32 minutes the vintage seaplane tender was underway, a little more than 28 hours after Amelia landed on Gardner Island. Steaming at full speed on a course of east southeast the 488-foot-long ship could cover the 1328 Nautical Miles in 3 days 16 hours and 32 minutes.

Lt. Commander Ohayashi received the following message from a very well placed agent who worked for Standard Oil at Luke Field on Ford Island, Pearl Harbor Hawaii. He was very adept at reporting all ship movements in and out of Pearl Harbor. This was quite easy because he had his Ham Radio Operator's license and a very elaborate radio setup.

FLASH

USS COLORADO WITH FULL
COMPLEMENT OF PLANES DEPARTED
PEARL HARBOR AT 1301 LOCAL TIME
JULY 3, 1937.

JULY 3, 1937

5:30 p.m. 23 hours and 15 minutes after
Earhart's disappearance
ONI Headquarters, Washington, D.C.

Things had now taken a turn for the worse at ONI
Headquarters because the cryptographers weren't
able to read the Blue code. They knew that someone
in Honolulu was transmitting, but they couldn't
decipher the text of the message. Giles filed the
following message from Lanning at 8:00 p.m. local
Washington D.C. time July 3rd.

TOP SECRET

**EYES ONLY: ASSISTANT CHIEF
BUREAU OF NAVIGATION**
LOST COMMO WITH JAPANESE, THEY
SWITCHED CODES. WE ARE FLYING BLIND
NOW, MUST RECOVER COVEY PLEASE
ADVISE NEW COURSE OF ACTION
SIGNED L

The U.S.S. *Colorado* left Pearl Harbor at 6 p.m. EST steering a course of south-southwest course. It could steam the 1808 nautical miles at its maximum speed of 21 knots in 3 days 14 hours and 6 minutes. The *Kamoi* had left Kwajalein at 10:32 p.m. EST and could make the trip to Gardner Island in 3 days 16 hours and 32 minutes. The race between the U.S.S. *Colorado* and Japanese Imperial Navy Ship *Kamoi* was on. The stakes couldn't have been higher.

The Cleveland Press

NIGHT EDITION

NAVY SEEKS AMELIA IN PACIFIC

Where Planes and Ships Seek Globe-Circling Flyers Lost in South Pacific

CLAIMS GERM OF PARALYSIS IS ISOLATED

AMATEURS GET HER SOS CALL

Ohio Crops Suffer Severe Damage From Heavy Rains

QUIET PREVAILS ON STEEL FRONT

UNION PACT ENDS GENERAL STRIKE

4 DETECTIVES HURT IN CRASH

CITY OBSERVES 3-DAY HOLIDAY

CHAPTER NINE

JULY 2, 1937

Day 1 Gardner Island

After resting for 20 minutes, Amelia wanted to busy herself with the business of survival and rescue. But, when she turned to face Fred, she noted his unfocused eyes and heard delusional, incoherent mutterings.

"Oh, no, Fred, Fred, can you understand me?" He didn't respond with anything that made sense. She inspected the deep gash on his head to find that although it had stopped bleeding, it was swollen and oozing. When they finally reached the beach, he slowly sagged onto the sand and fell into a deep, but troubled sleep. She found his whimpering and moaning very disturbing. She didn't know what other hidden injuries he sustained; she didn't have the expertise or the time to try to solve the mystery, either. Trying to make him as comfortable as possible, she put his rolled-up jacket under his head, immediately re-coiling at the tiny flies buzzing around and landing in the gaping wound.

She began to explore the immediate vicinity of

their landfall and by noon she had discovered the supplies left by the crew of the S.S. *Norwich City*. Although she felt encouraged by the sight of cans of food, some small tools and sundries, she was very disappointed to see lots of rust and mold encrusting the items. The bulk of it was unusable, especially the canned beans and fruit that were showing signs of spoilage. She thought, Damn, what a waste. The tops of those cans are so swollen, we'd be better off starving than eat that swill. She efficiently sorted the bounty, put aside what she thought was safe and walked back to the shoreline.

She noticed upon her return that the small waves lapping on the beach were beginning to move further up on the sand. The tide is coming in! Her thoughts went immediately to the *Electra* and her precious cargo of film. I better move the blasted film or the sea will snatch it. We risked everything to take those pictures. An A-5 magazine with 200 feet of film was heavy: 30 pounds each. She removed the magazine from the camera under Noonan's desk first, because the rising water was dangerously close to soaking the film. She walked to shore holding the magazine over her head and dropped it on the beach. Stretching backwards to ease her bruised, aching muscles, her gut tightened with anxiety when she started to face the reality of their situation. I better speed up or the *Electra* might wash into deeper water before I can finish. What am I going to do if Fred gets worse? When are we going to be rescued? GOD, I am *so* tired, but I can't stop now. She shook off her concerns and worked as quickly as possible. Grunting and perspiring profusely in the hot, moist heat of the tropics, she mused, thank goodness for small favors, these wing camera magazines are so much easier to deal with than the big one under the desk. Amelia waded in the four foot deep water to the shore holding the last magazine over her head. Several hours had passed, but she had managed to complete the task in spite of her fatigue and injuries. Sighing with relief, she muttered, "I better check on poor ole' Fred."

Nightfall came on the first night and while most people would have been sleeping after such a physically and mentally taxing day, Amelia was walking in calf deep water to her plane to fire up the radios and commence her broadcasts to the *Itasca*. She would begin her broadcasts with:

"KHAQQ CALLING NRU1, AMELIA EARHART CALLING NRU1, AMELIA EARHART CALLING *ITASCA* WE ARE ON AN UNCHARTED, SMALL UNIHABITED ISLAND AT L-A-T 4 DEGREES 40 MINUTES SOUTH L-O-N-G-174 DEGREES 32

MINUTES WEST ON A LINE 158.44 DEGREES
FROM TITUILA RADIO BEACON. THE PLANE
IS PARTIALY ON LAND PART IN WATER. MY
NAVIGATOR FRED NOONAN IS SERIOUSLY
INJURED WE NEED HELP IMMEDIATELY. I
ALSO HAVE INJURIES BUT NOT AS BAD AS MR.
NOONAN." She would transmit this message and
then wait for a reply. Hopeful of quick results, she
repeated this message over and over from 7:15 p.m.
until 10:30 p.m. that night. She ran the right engine
to recharge the battery. Amelia knew that she had
landed with about 60 gallons of fuel in the wing
tanks. This would give her 9 to 10 hours of time to
broadcast to the outside world. Was that really the
Itasca? Thank God! Amelia thought. She happily
assumed it was when the radio crackled alive with a
request for her to broadcast 4 dashes. At least that's
what she thought she heard. She complied by keying
the mike to simulate 4 long dashes for the next hour
at 15-minute intervals. No matter how tired she was,
the ship *Itasca* was always foremost on her mind.
She re-visited previous conversations as her attention
wandered from the monotonous task. They assured
me over and over that the *Itasca's* captain would know
our plan. If Noonan and I couldn't find Howland Island,
we would fly to Gardner Island and await rescue. Every

detail was worked out; it all sounded so simple then. Nothing else could go wrong, could it?

This strategy would have been a very simple solution to their problem. But, things were not as they appeared to be. What Amelia didn't know was Commander Thompson of the *Itasca* had *no* knowledge of her intentions to fly to Gardner Island! He assumed she was floating northwest of Howland Island and had rushed to her rescue there. ONI *still had not* informed the *Itasca* commander of the full plan for many reasons. Mostly it was due to concerns of secrecy and national security. Also, the President could hardly deny Earhart's intentions if she was ever caught flying over a secret Japanese installation a thousand miles off course *and* taking pictures, no less! Hard to cover up a gaff like that, especially when a famed aviator was involved. No, the government felt secrecy was the way to proceed, even if it came down to a choice between her and war with Japan: the U.S. had to stay out of a war. To make matters worse, she did not realize she was actually *on* Gardner Island! Purposely, she had given only their presumed coordinates and avoided the words *Gardner Island*. This was to prevent the possibility of the *Itasca* steaming to Gardner Island and not finding them there.

Knowing it would take the *Itasca* two days to get

to them made Amelia feel a little despondent, but practical matters had to take precedent over any pity party. She was exhausted and rapidly becoming disheartened, but she turned her attention to the matter of food and water. The cans of condensed milk from the *Norwich*'s supplies will cheer Fred up a bit. I just can't believe there is no fresh water on this God-forsaken piece of sand. At least we'll have some liquid. Too bad there were only a few cans safe enough to drink. I don't want to think about what will happen when the milk runs out. I haven't seen a coconut, either. Maybe I can set up a rain catcher in case we're lucky enough to have some rain. If only I had some canvas. Another thing we had to leave behind. She gazed at the sky wistfully and saw only a beautiful, clear sunshiny day. Vivid shades of blue surrounded her in a vast, gorgeous panorama that she failed to appreciate at this time.

Noonan was a burden, just when she didn't need another one. Amelia checked his head wound again and used sea water to clean out the wound as much as possible. At least the flies are gone for a while, but it looks like it's getting infected. It's so swollen. Hmm, I wonder what else I can do for him? He winced in fitful sleep and his babbling intensified. "Marie, that hurts so much! Why are you hurting me?" Then he started to rave incoherently, getting louder and louder. Concerned, Amelia pondered, why he is saying Marie? Wasn't his new wife's name Mary? He must have a very high temperature. What I wouldn't give to have some aspirin or pain killers. Let me add that to my wish list.

Another problem presented itself the first night. She stumbled to the plane to try to make contact again. It was a coal black night, so dark she could hardly see her hands in front of her. Crabs, night creatures, rocks and debris littered her way. She broadcasted on 3105, her night time frequency, but the flashlight was getting dimmer.

She shook the flashlight and spoke aloud to the *Electra,* "I don't think the batteries will last another night. We left the extra batteries at Lae to save weight, but that's spilled milk, old gal. I'll pretty much have to transmit in daylight from now on." Once the batteries failed she didn't want to take the chance of getting lost in the dark on her way to and from the aircraft. Amelia had maintained her cool the first night even though there still was no answer to her four dashes.

She made it back to where Noonan lay asleep on the sand and fell into a fitful sleep moments after lying down. Coconut crabs awoke her several times when they clamped onto her toes. "Fred. Fred?" No answer. The rats were beginning to present a problem, she felt their presence even in the pitch black of the tropical night. Noonan awoke many times during night angry at their situation and fending off the imaginary rat attacks. Or were they imaginary? The quarter moon rose just after 2 a.m. and she could see the red eyes staring at her from the bushes on the perimeter of their camp.

JULY 3, 1937

Day 2 on Gardner Island

It dawned at 6:17 a.m. and while a weary Amelia was doing everything she could to comfort her partner, the Japanese ship *Kamoi* was heading for their island. She gave him a cheery, "good morning" and a gentle hug. Fred was having a rare moment of clarity. They chatted quietly and recounted all the past events to try and make sense out of them. Why didn't anyone answer? They shared a can of condensed milk and some canned meat she opened with a screwdriver that she had found in the *Norwich City* cache. "Not very good, but enough to keep us going," Fred said, trying to be pleasant. "I feel a little better today…"

Clunk! He passed out suddenly and hit his head on a large shell. His wound re-opened and started to bleed again. Amelia quickly went to work cleaning and wrapping it with the salt-water-soaked piece of shirt that had been on it before. She alternated a rag and that cloth as that's all she had. It was 8 a.m. when she made her way in the ankle deep surf to the *Electra,* which didn't seem damaged after it's time in four and a half feet of water at high tide. The radios functioned well, but she still heard no response after broadcasting for two and a half hours. Amelia reasoned that she could transmit and listen on 3105 and then switch to 6210 and repeat the process. She felt certain that the *Itasca* was at least half way between Howland and her location, and they would be listening to one or both of her frequencies. For the trillionth time, why wouldn't they answer?

By 10 a.m., the temperature in the cockpit of the *Electra* was above 90 degrees. The air was still because the prevailing wind was right off the nose of the aircraft. There was no way to achieve cross ventilation and Amelia rapidly became limp from the stifling heat, humidity and near dehydration. Up to this time she had taken little more than small sips of their precious milk thus giving Fred the lion's share because he was so weak. She heard carrier waves several times, sounds made when someone was transmitting on the frequency, but no voices came through. The right engine was running off and on recharging the batteries. Several times while listening for some human sound, her mind drifted. The trip was so much fun until everything started to go wrong on this leg. Annoyed with herself, she shook herself back to reality when she realized that her situation wasn't changed from the day before. Amelia continued to broadcast for another twenty minutes after shutting the engine down. But still no one answered her call for help. She spent another hour looking through Noonan's notes and getting the map case loose from his desk. Ahhh, my ribs ache. This case is really heavy. Fred must have been stronger than he looked. She lugged the case containing the charts and sextant back to shore. She hoped Fred would snap out of his delirium and help her figure out where they were. If I could broadcast a name for the island, then the *Itasca* would know right where to come for us. My lips are so dry. She put down the burden and rubbed her face. When she touched her lips she cried out in pain. "Water, I need to find some water." She begged God for a tall, cool drink of water, something good to eat and the pain to subside from her lips, bruised areas and sore ribs.

She spent the rest of the day methodically comb-
ing their sandy prison for water and sustenance. So
far other than sampling the foul stagnant water from
small pools, she had no success with finding liquid or
any signs of life other than vegetation and creatures
that crawled, flew or swam. Then the coconut game
began. "Wow," she told the island, "look at all those
trees. So many coconuts! We are saved! I can't wait
to drink the milk. I hope Fred can chew the inside,
because I know I can." She managed to gather a few
and threw the loose ones up at the top of the tall, tall
trees to dislodge more. She brought what she could
carry back to the camp. Then she emptied Fred's
aluminum chart case. Fred was still sleeping, so she
found her way back to the coconut grove. As she
made the trek it dawned on her that the case would
make a decent pot for boiling the stagnant water
that she had found earlier. She filled his case with
her new-found treasure and lugged the fruit back to
her temporary home. Exhausted, but very thirsty, she
started to work on a coconut. This is going to be soo
good, she thought in expectation.

Five hours after she had commenced surgery
on her first coconut, she had managed by trial and
error to accumulate enough pulp to feed them for a
while. Unfortunately, she had extracted only enough

milk to sustain them for short time. Island natives with machetes made the process look so easy when they lopped the tops off with one swift whack. Amelia struggled mightily with the outer husks, smashing with hard coral rocks, gouging with her precious screwdriver over and over until she found a process that worked. And it took arduous hours of labor to produce enough liquid to just keep them alive in the heat of the tropics. Dehydration was always a short time away, day or night.

Just as the sun was setting, she again waded through the calf-deep water to the *Electra.* The tide was on its way out and this would give her about 3 hours of broadcasting before she would have to make her way back to shore. At 7 p.m. she started the right engine and turned on the radios and cockpit lights to save what little life that was left in her flashlight. She tuned the low frequency radio to KGMB out of Honolulu, the strongest broadcasting station in the Pacific, just to hear another human voice. She began her tasks of trying to reach someone broadcasting, listening and switching frequencies. Running the engine to recharge the battery and shutting it down to save fuel was also part of her busy night. She broadcasted the same message with little deviation over and over again with no response. Her eyes were starting to droop, her injuries and the lack of a response, both from Fred and the *Itasca,* were beginning to wear down her indomitable spirit. I have to stay strong. If I fall apart now it's all over for Fred and me. I can't believe I am in this position. I thought we planned for any contingency. Then at 9 p.m. her heart almost leaped out of her chest. "Calling Amelia Earhart, Calling Amelia Earhart, please listen to KGMB 1320 kHz at 10 o'clock and transmit on 3105, 6210 or 500. If you receive this message please respond with two long dashes." Hearing her name over the radio made her as giddy as a school girl. She realized that the navy was using the powerful civilian radio station to get her a message. Three minutes later she keyed the mike twice to answer when she realized they had left their Morse code key back in Miami. In the future I will only transmit on 3105, since it seems to give the best results, she decided.

At 10 p.m. her DF receiver was tuned to 1320 kHz and true to their word KGMB sent her a message. "Calling Amelia Earhart, Calling Amelia Earhart. If you hear this transmission, respond with 2 dashes if you are on the water and three dashes if you are on land." She responded by keying the mike three times. The radio vigil ended at 1130 p.m. when the rising tide made running the engine impossible. Her trusty flashlight finally gave up the fight halfway to shore and she finished the trek by starlight.

The second night on the island was spent in a fitful sleep fending off snapping coconut crabs. Rats scurried closer, ever closer. The bolder ones led the others into their little camp, sniffing and scratching around their clothes and supplies. They lit a fire with Noonan's lighter, but she couldn't depend on him to gather wood to keep it going. He was sinking lower and lower into a state of debilitating depression and constant pain. Sleep was his only respite. Several times during the night he woke up calling, "Marie, Marie, where are you? Help meeeeee."

The next day would be the fourth of July. That was the day her husband, George Putnam, had arranged several elaborate events for her arrival in Oakland. Amelia lay half-awake listening to the soothing, but sometimes creepy critter sounds on their tiny Pacific island. Her mind traveled into the near future. I was supposed to be the guest of honor at all the grand parties. Oh yes, Fred too. The parties are not to be because I failed in my mission to fly around the earth. No parties with tables brimming with delicious food. Sigh. She smiled to herself and thought, Well, I do have mystery meat. And there would have been drinks, too! I bet they wouldn't have served warm canned milk or coconut milk. She missed her husband and her life at home. Lonely and alone in the middle of a vast ocean, she felt a heavy pressure bearing down on her chest. Her whole being ached with longing. She did have her sick friend, a well renowned and respected navigator. Fred is such a talented and brilliant man. It's scary to see him this way. His brain is like mush. Wow, how wonderful would it be if we were rescued on the 4th of July! America would be 161 years old and all our troubles would be over. The *Itasca* should be close tomorrow, was her last pleasant thought before falling into a short fitful sleep.

Memories of the good life she left behind.

CHAPTER TEN

JULY 4, 1937

Day 3 on Gardner Island

She was filled with optimism and she just knew that today was the day. The warm canned milk and nasty canned meat didn't taste as bad as it had over the last 2 days. Little did she know that the *Itasca* was not on the way to the Phoenix Islands as she hoped. It was actually headed to a search area due west of Howland. Unbelievably, Commander Thompson was still under the impression that the aircraft had landed on the water and was floating. Also, several radio intercepts that were at first thought to be from the *Electra*, were actually the *Itasca* attempting to contact Amelia! EXCEPT FOR THE THREE DASHES RECEIVED BY FT. SHAFTER AFTER THE KGMB BROADCAST INDICATING THAT SHE WAS ON LAND, ALL OTHER COMMUNICATIONS WERE A BUNDLE OF CONFUSION ABOUT WHO SENT WHAT MESSAGE! Amelia would have been horrified that none of the efforts were coordinated and were in many cases working at cross purposes. But she didn't know: ignorance can be bliss. The botched search efforts were snowballing at every turn. Fred and Amelia were paying a heavy price for governmental bureaucracy at its worst.

She decided to skip the morning radio report because her results last night had been so good. She happily trotted to the northwest tip of the island to see if she could catch sight of the *Itasca* coming over the horizon. Amelia sat on the beach for a half hour before she decided to explore the other side of the island. Except for the reef being much smaller and the absence of the S.S. *Norwich City*, the north side of the island was pretty much the same as the southern side. Upon getting a closer look at the lagoon she realized that it was full of circling small, but seemingly vicious sharks. Look at those teeth! Not a place to go swimming or get fresh drinking water. I didn't notice any sharks on the way to and from the plane. I better be more cautious tonight.

Noonan was still sleeping when she returned three hours later. She made the same old lunch of warm milk and canned meat. She hammered away at a few coconuts, but tired quickly. "A little salt and pepper would go a long way, but fat chance." she said aloud. Fred stirred and said "Pass the salt, would you, Marie. I'm starving." She moved closer. "Fred. Fred, are you feeling any better?" No answer. Amelia just looked at him and then her stomach growled. She sighed and dug into her feast.

She spent the rest of the afternoon writing in her journal about the happenings of the last 4 days. She had neglected her journal since they took off from Lae. The trip to Truk and back to their original course left no time for writing. She had to focus constantly, there was no relief. Fred was no help and was becoming more and more of a burden. Will Fred still be alive when help arrives? She dared not think *if* help arrives. Night time wasn't the time to write, nor had she felt like writing about missing Howland and not being able to find Gardner Island. God, have you abandoned us? Will we die on this island? I am so confused and doggone tired. I'm still hungry. She had spent the first two days trying to get Noonan's head wound doctored, finding food and establishing contact with the outside world: not much success on any of the projects. They had no fresh water and were rapidly running out of the little milk and food she had found. The coconuts were a mixed blessing: nourishing, but difficult to deal with. Now she had no flashlight. Things were looking bleaker by the minute. She had trouble focusing on the journal, so she didn't

note anything but pertinent facts about their predicament, just the cold, hard facts. On some level
she knew any emotional outpouring might bring her
dismal mood even lower.

Amelia slowly walked to the crippled *Electra* just
before sunset. At least she could see the sand through
the surf as she crossed the water. The setting sun
shimmered on the shallow water. She was grateful
for the light breeze as her heavy shirt was hot on her
body. Even though she was fuzzy from fatigue, she
was mindful of sharks. She sat in the cockpit and
mulled over in her mind what to say. Noonan had kept
a log of all his calculations. She made a mental note
to go through it page by page tomorrow morning and
try to figure out where they were. The right engine
roared to life at 6:15 p.m. She began her attempt to
make positive contact with the *Itasca*. Please, God,
let me hear a response tonight. I don't know how
long we can hang on. She rubbed the back of her
neck repeatedly to loosen up that tight area between
her shoulder blades. Finally, at 6:30 p.m. a call came
through KGMB. "Calling Amelia Earhart, Calling
Amelia Earhart, listen for call at 0630 Greenwich Mean
Time." The message was repeated every five minutes
until 7 p.m. her time and then came the message.
"Amelia Earhart, turn on your transmitter for one

minute for tuning purposes and then send 4 dashes if you hear KGMB and wait for our acknowledgment." She froze for a split second and then did precisely as instructed: Click...click...click...click..., four one-second long dashes. It was a long, tortuous three minutes. Then KGMB repeated the message and she again responded. KGMB then broadcasted. "Key your mike four times if you are north of Howland Island, six if you are south. Key your mike twice if you are on land and three times if you are on water."

She was stunned. "Oh Lord, they don't know we are south of Howland!" She whispered. Then, "Why don't they know about Gardner?" she screamed into the dark night. Her heart pounding, nausea rising, she felt faint. She swiveled sideways in her pilot's chair and lowered her head between her knees. Does this mean that none of our position reports had gotten out? Her mind raced faster and faster until thoughts were spewing from her brain. Was the *Itasca* actually on its way? Didn't the captain know about her plan to go south? These horrendously shocking revelations over-powered her for a few minutes and for the first time she was truly frightened. Like the crashed Wall Street stocks of 1929, her survival futures just plummeted.

She took a deep breath and forced herself to focus on the immediate task. She had to respond carefully,

very carefully. After all, she knew that their survival piv-
oted on each and every transmission. She had to get
this right, dead right. "Dammit," she said to the radio
in an uncharacteristic show of extreme frustration. She
sighed and tried to force her mind to focus, What had
they asked for......four dashes if south of Howland
or was it north and was it six south......"Calm down
Amelia," she whispered to herself. She waited for the
repeat broadcast. Should I combine the dashes or wait
between them, why couldn't they be more specific?
She took a chance and keyed the mike eight times,
south and on land, but would they get that? She spent
the next three seeming endless hours making her
position reports and keying the mike eight times. At
10:30 p.m. she shut down her engine and finished the
last transmission of the night at 10:47. Amelia gave no
thought to the sharks as she slowly plodded in water
over her knees to the shore. She was more than shaken
by the night's events. It was a moonless night and she
stumbled through the total void. She was light-footed
when she moved to check on Noonan. Thankfully,
he was quiet and still breathing. Then she realized he
had hardly eaten anything all day. But then, she hadn't
either. Earlier they had gathered some more coconuts
and palm fronds when Fred was in one of his lucid
moments. She began to build a fire and found that the

plentiful coconut husks and palm fronds burned nicely. By 11 p.m. the short dancing flames were offering her a little bit of warmth and comfort. But they did little to ward off the freezing gusts of fear blowing, always blowing. If, and that is an enormous if, her messages were received and understood correctly, it would take a minimum of two days for a ship to reach them. She worried and thought maybe the ship is at Gardner and can't find this place. She was too exhausted to go on and fell into a fitful, hungry and thirsty sleep. It was slumber that came with rat and crab infestation and the same old thoughts playing and re-playing in her head. What would the morning bring, it was impossible to say?

America's ineptitude of the moment didn't extend to the Japanese at the Naval Secret Police Headquarters at Kwajalein. The high command had been very busy and seemed to know what they were doing. Lieutenant Commanders Ohayashi and Sato, leaders of the Radio Intercept and Intelligence sections had instructed their radio operators to begin playing music on 3105 and key their mikes whenever they suspected a transmission from the downed *Electra*. This would partially block out her transmissions because their transmitters were more powerful. They also keyed the mike at random with any combination of dashes except eight long ones. By midnight on the night of the 4th of July, the two Japanese officers had put together and translated, as best they could, a message that would be sent within the next hour.

Noonan awoke sobbing and calling for Marie again. Amelia's eyes were half closed, her body was wracked with pain and her endurance was depleted by exhaustion and dehydration. Despite all that, she kindly, if halfheartedly tried to comfort him with platitudes. Her spirit was severely weakened as she realized she had little control over her life. Cracks were beginning to form in her indomitable spirit. Since July 2, 1937 Amelia Earhart had become the prize in a race. The competitors were the Japanese, who seemed to know their business and were running flat out, and the Americans who had chosen secrecy and caution over speed.

JULY 5, 1939

Lieutenant Commanders Ohayashi and Sato had

finally formulated the message that was be sent by 2 a.m. the latest. The effort had taken several hours. They had written the message in Japanese and had a very difficult time translating it into English. By 12:30 a.m. local time they had finished it and gave it to the intercept section to be transmitted in Morse code. What they failed to realize was the operators in the section didn't speak English and had a very difficult time transmitting the message. Neither Amelia nor Fred were proficient at Morse code so it would actually appear that they had sent the bogus message: very bad luck for the doomed pair. The message was short, to the point and sent very haltingly.

> TWO EIGHT ONE MILES NORTH OF HOWLAND, CALL KHAQQ WHEN BEYOND HOWLAND TO NORTH, DO NOT HOLD BACK, LUCK NOT WITH US MUCH LONGER, WE ARE ABOVE WATER, MUST SHUT OFF RADIO NOW.

The three operators on duty at 2 a.m. on the morning of July 5th at U.S. Navy Radio Station Wailupe received the message. They had a very difficult time getting the message due to static and the very poor

Morse code transmission. They couldn't get it in its entirety, therefore the message they received has never made sense, then or now.

> TWO EIGHT ONE NORTH HOWLAND, CALL KHAQQ BEYOND NORTH, DON'T HOLD WITH US MUCH LONGER ABOVE WATER, SHUT OFF.

. . . .

Even though the message made little sense, it shot through the searchers' network like a bolt of lightning in a summer thunderstorm. Commander Thompson ordered the *Itasca* to make all haste to the ocean 281 miles north of Howland Island. The USS *Swan* and S.S. *Moorsby*, a British merchant ship, quickly joined the party. The search continued until July 5th when a message was received from Lockheed that the *Electra* could only transmit if it had landed wheels down on land. Also, that evening Pan American told the Coast Guard that all their radio intercepts pointed to the British-held Phoenix Islands. At 9:12 the evening of July 5th, after mistaking heat lightening for flares from Amelia, the *Itasca* gave up the search of the area

281 miles north of Howland! They then began preparing to rendezvous with the USS *Colorado* to refuel at sea.

Lieutenant Commander's Ohayashi Radio Intercept section had accomplished their mission. He had used the radios that were set up to monitor signals from Hawaii. The antennas were directed at Hawaii so only Hawaii had heard the message. U.S. Radio Wailupe had no high frequency DF so they couldn't tell where the message came from! That was another lucky break for Ohayashi and Sato because they didn't know about the U.S.'s ability to Direction Find high frequency traffic. Their ruse had bought 36 hours' extra time for Japanese Captain Kozaka on the seaplane tender, *Kamoi*, to win the race to Gardner Island. The famous lost Americans marooned on Gardner had no way of knowing about the drama that was being played on the high seas of the Pacific. At last something was going their way. The *Kamoi* had old boilers that defied the full speed ahead orders that Captain Kozaka gave his crew. The *Kamoi's* engine room officer was forced to throttle back to 10 knots per hour at the half way point to Gardner Island. This set back their arrival time at Gardner by approximately 24 hours.

JULY 5, 1939

Day 4 on Gardner Island

When the light was bright enough to read, Amelia was at work trying to glean as much as she possibly could from Noonan's notes and scribblings on his charts. She would try to give as much information as possible today over the radio because time was running out. Although their breakfast fare was unpleasant and their diet never varied, she and Noonan ate hungrily. After the disappointments of last night, Amelia was even more determined to do everything in her power to accomplish a rescue, whatever it took.

It was 8:30 and the morning sun was already glaring down on her bare head when she sloshed through the ankle deep water to the plane. "Come on Fred, try and carry your own weight around here. Get the lead out." After the harsh words flew out of her mouth, she was sorry. "Fred, I know you are weak but I really, really need your help today. Please try and understand me." No answer from Fred. She had an added burden for this morning's trek over the reef. She had to half carry, half drag Noonan with her. He had not been at the campsite this morning when she woke up, so she promptly went looking for him. She found him at the mouth of the lagoon near the SS *Norwich City* drinking water from a small pool formed by an eddy. Amelia tasted the water and immediately spit it out, it was sea water! That could account for some of the delirium he was suffering. "How long have you been drinking from this pool?" she demanded. He ignored her until she pulled him out of the pool. "On your feet, Fred, I can't leave you alone anymore!" Her exasperation showed by the scowl she wore as she led him to the plane.

Amelia broke her daily routine of calling the *Itasca* and began by broadcasting to anyone who would listen.

"This is Amelia Earhart calling. This is Amelia Earhart calling. We are on an uninhabited, uncharted island, my navigator is badly injured, we need medical help! Please help us." Her voice today was more of a plea than the crisp professional one heard over the last three days. After finishing the call, she would wait a minute or two for a response, then she would repeat the message. Suddenly she gasped when the radio crackled in response.

"W4OK calling Amelia Earhart, W4OK calling Amelia Earhart, over."

This was one the few voices she had heard, other than Fred's, since she landed on this "island paradise." Her heart was pounding.

"W4OK we are on a one five eight, three three eight line from Tutuila Radio. Tutuila is 158.44 degrees, repeat Tutuila is 158.44 degrees. Please help me, the water gets high at night......"

"Have you got someone?" Noonan interrupted

"Yes, here put it up to your ear!"

"This is Amelia Putnam, this is Amelia Earhart Putnam Please help us, SOS...Stop it..." This time Noonan had grabbed the microphone from her hand and began to ramble. Speak to me, Uncle Sam, speak to me. Oh, no, you can't leave us here......" He began to sob and relaxed his grip on the microphone.

"Help, help us quick..." she said as Noonan continued babbling through his tears.

"It's so hot, so hot in here, I have to get out!"

"I can feel it, the heat, you are right, we have a job..." Amelia said with the radio still in the transmit position. "Come here just a moment, please get back in the aircraft." But Noonan wouldn't listen, so she climbed out the escape hatch and down the wing to where he stood with tears in his eyes. She looked over at him and was instantly struck by his appearance. What a sad, pitiful man he had become. I always knew you to be a strong, highly intelligent and clear-headed man, Fred. That is what she thought, but she said softly, "Fred, please calm down and come with me. Let's go back to the plane. Someone is on the radio and they will help us, you'll see."

"We're lost, we're lost," he said, consigning both of them to their fate. But Amelia refused to allow him to give up. She knew that if he gave in she would probably follow suit shortly. Then they would both be lost. She got him back into the cockpit with great effort as her strength was beginning to flag. She then tried to raise W4OK again.

"We are on an uninhabited, uncharted island on a 338/158 line from Tutuila Radio. We think we're in the Phoenix Islands, send us help, send us help."

"Amelia take it, I can't hear...take it...help... help, I need air, it is so hot in here. Amelia, things are hopeless...Here I come Marie, here I come...Oh my god my head hurts so bad, so bad......let me out of here......it's so different......suffer, suffer that is all I'm doing......Take it away I don't want to be here anymore." Noonan was uncontrollable. His jabbering was beginning to get on Amelia's nerves, which were on edge anyway. She tried to override him by speaking loudly over his background noise.

"We heard WGMB last night, please broadcast again." Reading from Noonan's notes, "South 3 degrees 09 minutes 165 degrees east. Please help us. We need medical assistance soon, can't hold out much longer. Norwich City, Norwich City, Norwich City, we are at the Norwich City." Her voice was starting to crack from dryness and nerves. Noonan left the aircraft four times and each time she had to shut down the right engine because she feared he might walk into the propeller. "My head, my head, my head. Make it stop hurting, Marie. I'm hotttttt......" He yelled, his voice trailing behind him as he ran away again.

"'Hot, so hot," she barely heard him yell over the roar of the engine. This time she let him go, consequences be damned. She was getting desperate. She continued reading all the figures in his notes that looked pertinent. She had no idea if anyone was receiving her transmissions since the time she had talked to W4OK. Amazingly enough, W4OK was a ham radio operator in Palm Beach, Florida. At the beginning of her conversation, he had answered her three times. She was able to pass on a personal message to her husband through this man in Florida. This was very important to Amelia. "Tell my husband, George, to get the suitcase in my closet in California." She was attempting to tell her husband in code to destroy secret papers in the zipper part of her briefcase. In actuality, her briefcase was filled with information about what had occurred on the Matson ship, USS *Lurline*, sailing from California to Honolulu in 1934. She and her husband had been on the ship with Paul Mantz and his wife before her Honolulu to California flight. What happened in 1934 on the USS *Lurline* is still a mystery to this day. She sincerely hoped he would get this message and carry out her wishes. Unbeknownst to her, the ham operator did call the coast guard and been assured that ships were closing in on her location. They thanked him for his concern.

She shut down the right engine and kept transmitting until the radio battery was almost dead. It was 11 o'clock in the morning when the tide was to a point that precluded her operating the right engine anymore. When the water rose to two feet, the whirling propeller would hit the water and probably damage the blades and engine. Not noticing the multitude of sea gulls ravaging the decayed crabs and intense heat, she made her way back to the campsite trying to decide what to do about Fred and the problem with the sea water. Boy, am I thirsty, but I'm just too tired to attack the coconuts. Hmm, I probably won't get much sleep tonight as I have to stand guard over Fred. I heard people can go mad when they drink sea water. Maybe I'll give him a double portion of the canned milk to cut down his thirst and get some of that stagnant water. She sighed from exhaustion and resigned herself to the fact that Fred would need constant vigilance.

They ate their regular meal. Even though Amelia was very dehydrated, she gave her ration of milk to Fred. Earlier she had fetched water from the shallow pools that had not fully dried up since the last rainfall. But, her only large container, Fred's chart case, leaked out all the water before she could get it back to camp. Her mind was not as clear as it had been a few days earlier due to mental and physical exhaustion. She was only aware that she was making many mistakes. When people reach their breaking point, they usually know what they are doing wrong, but they don't have the physical or mental capabilities at that time to reverse the trend. In other words, they are close to giving up.

She spent the next two radio sessions on the night of the 5th and the morning of the 6th broadcasting the same information she had been giving out for the last four days.

JULY 6, 1937

Day 5 Gardner Island

The day passed without incident except Amelia tried her luck at noodling (catching fish by grabbing them with bare hands). Up to this point she had not had much luck with any other method she had tried. The effort was not worth it, because all she ever got were small fish with what seemed like more bone than flesh. She had roasted some crabs on their fire, but Fred refused both the fish and the crab. All that work catching the fish and he won't eat it, she resentfully reflected. Why do I bother? I guess I am fonder of him than I thought. Mary will kill me if I don't bring him back safe and sound. I'm glad I saved some of that fish oil I squeezed out of those little critters. My sunburn is hurting real bad and the salt water is still stinging. Palm trees don't give off much shade and they had no tarps as they had only taken the bare-bone necessities in order to lighten the aircraft.

Licking her swollen, chapped lips Amelia made her way to the plane for the last time that evening. Gas for the right engine was about gone and she knew that this was the last chance to raise someone. It had been four and a half days since they had landed on the reef and she had only made contact with one station. She hoped that when the operator of station W4OK gave her messages to the Coast Guard and that they would rescue them. The uncharted deserted island seemed more and more inhospitable every day.

"This is Amelia Earhart calling, this is Amelia Earhart calling, can you read me, can you read me? This is Amelia Earhart, this is Amelia Earhart, please come in. We are at latitude four degrees forty minutes south, longitude one seventy-four degrees thirty-two minutes west, repeat, latitude four degrees forty minutes south, longitude one seventy four degrees thirty- two minutes west. We have taken in water and my navigator is badly hurt, repeat, we have taken in water and my navigator is badly hurt. We are in need of medical care and must have help; we can't hold on much longer."

The Japanese had resorted to playing music on this station on a 24-hour basis so reception was iffy at best. This message was heard by Thelma Landstille who lived in St. Stephens, New Brunswick, Canada, but her husband, Lyle, assured her that it was only a radio program. "After all, Earhart has been missing a week, eh, it couldn't possibly be her." It was 8:28 P.M on Amelia's watch when the right engine ran out of fuel and at 8:47 p.m. the radio battery went dead for the last time. As she returned to the shore splashing in the ankle-deep water her spirits were at an all-time low. She had never felt like this before.

"Get rid of all the excess weight you can before you take off from Lae!" had been the mantra of Kelly Johnson and Paul Mantz before she and Noonan left from the Skunk Works in Burbank. We heeded the advice maybe a little too zealously, she thought. Gone were their parachutes which would have been very useful as shelter against the relentless sun. She had left most of her toiletries behind. Oh, what she wouldn't give for some toothpaste and a toothbrush. No extra food or water and the rubber raft would have caught a lot of rain during yesterday's downpour. Not one of them had thought about what would happen if they weren't picked up in two days or less. If the truth were known, all good pilots make alternate plans to land if their primary airport becomes unavailable. The primary concern is a safe landing. She had even left the First-Aid kit behind. Their plight didn't seem to be improving, despite her best efforts. Her thoughts returned to the present, she couldn't do anything about the past.

Fred Noonan was out of his head from his injury and consumption of salt water. She had trouble keeping up with his erratic behavior. One minute he seemed lucid, the next he was uttering nonsense. There was a cup of rain water left from what she had caught yesterday during a short, but welcomed downpour. The canned milk was gone except for 2 cans and the food supply was almost gone. The lighter was out of fluid so there was no more chance of a fire, the wood supply was wet from the rain yesterday, anyway. The radio to the outside world was finished and she had only talked to one person. If they weren't rescued soon, she felt they would die of thirst within a week. The coconuts were becoming more and more of a tease as she became too weak to fight with their outer husks. She resolved to make Fred comfortable as long as possible. Amelia still had hope, but it was a dim flame very deep inside her. When she fell asleep that night she didn't pay any attention to the crabs, rats or Noonan's ravings. She was tired to the bone, depressed and her injuries hurt worse than they had the day of the landing. The around the world flight was a very distant memory of better times.

JULY 7, 1937

Washington, D.C.

The Man from ONI checked his message traffic from the Chief of Naval Operations Pacific and wasn't very pleased. It was just after noon as he looked at the position of the USS *Colorado*. That damned ship should be at Gardner Island by now, but it was reported to be only 200 miles northwest of Howland Island refueling the *Itasca*. From the looks of things they are still 600 miles from Gardner Island. If it steamed at 25 knots it would make it by the morning of July 8th. Oh, well, that should suffice as I don't feel it's wise to tell the Chief of Naval Operations to have the USS *Colorado* steam with all possible speed to Gardner. That would put too much emphasis on Gardner and that might give away ONI's involvement with the mission. His misguided concerns were a very real consideration, after all, they didn't want the Japanese to know that ONI had pictures of Truk.

JULY 7, 1937

Japanese Command at Kwajalein

The Japanese were anxiously waiting for an urgent communication because they hadn't gotten the code word enclosed in Captain Kozaka's sealed orders. The word was to be broadcasted once the *Kamoi* picked up Earhart and her navigator and the ship was on its way back to Kwajalein. Assuming the worst, as was his nature, Kozaka, hadn't been able to tell Headquarters of his need to slow his speed because of the radio silence order. This race, converging on Gardner Island with Amelia, Fred and some very sought after photographs, was drawing to a close. A hungry, thirsty, and totally perplexed Amelia was approaching the end of her endurance. Captain Kozaka of the *Kamoi* was carrying the hopes of the Empire of Japan with him. Nevertheless, he had started to exercise caution to avoid burning out his engines.

JULY 7, 1937

200 miles northwest of Howland Island

Lacking orders to the contrary, Captain W.L. Friedell, commander of the USS *Colorado*, was also proceeding with extreme caution. He was carrying the hopes of The Man from ONI and the President. Everyone was being cautious, but sometimes caution can be extremely dangerous.

Imperial Japanese Navy seaplane tender Kamoi capable of hoisting a Lockheed Electra aboard.

CHAPTER ELEVEN

JULY 7, 1937

Day 6 on Gardner Island

It was 10:14 a.m. according to Noonan's chronometers and they finished the last vestige of their simple fare. They had long ago swallowed the last of the milk and eaten all of the stringy canned beef. Her night had again been a series of short naps because the crawling pests. Debris was strewn around their small camp because the rats had been digging away at the buried beef and milk tins. She shivered when she momentarily re-lived the feel and scent of them as they crawled over her in the night.

She was walking towards the beach that morning when she stopped in her tracks. In the distance from the northwest she thought she heard an aircraft engine. At first she thought it was her imagination because it was her greatest wish to hear one. Several times in the last two days she had wanted a dinner of lamb chops and roasted potatoes so bad she swore she could smell it cooking. The smell always evaporated quickly, but this time the sound of the engine grew louder. Amelia broke into a run to the beach and within five minutes a seaplane appeared just above the horizon!

"We're saved, thank God, we're saved!" she yelled as if someone were there to listen.

Her injuries and fatigue were briefly erased as the soft sand tried to hold her back with every step. Even when her legs began to ache she ran on like a school girl just let out for the holidays. She got to the beach just before the aircraft approached the reef's edge. Her heart was beating wildly, both from excitement and exertion as the approaching aircraft headed straight for her, approximately 100 feet above the water. She felt heady from the adrenalin rush when she saw that it was a green bi-winged seaplane with a large float below the fuselage and a float under each wing. As it flew over her head her joy suddenly turned to horror as she saw the large red circles trimmed in white under the wing. She whispered to herself, "the Imperial Japanese Navy emblem." The pilot and radio operator waved as they made the low pass and she waved back, but not with much enthusiasm. How had this happened? Where was the *Itasca*? She waved back as they made low pass after low pass and finally turned toward the northwest and headed away. She knew they were returning to their ship, which was most likely just over the horizon. There was no time to lose. Her body screamed at the sudden forceful exertion as she ran back to their camp. Amelia's mind was working faster than it had since her first day on the island. She had only an hour at the most before they would be here and she had a lot to do.

Luckily for Amelia, Captain Kozaka decided to steam to the island confident that there was no reason to send more aircraft, after all why keep track of people that weren't going anywhere. Amelia carried the film magazines to a high point hidden in the low brush under the trees, about 200 yards from their campsite. The effort was monumental as it was hot and she had nothing left to drink except a little water from the rain two days ago. Her injuries came alive to let her know they were not completely healed. She ignored their cry for her to slow down. It was close to a half an hour before she had the three heavy magazines on the small hill. She began to dig furiously in the sand until she reached lava rock about 2 feet down. The sand had started to get moist just before she reached rock. The hiding place was well chosen. Was there fresh water? Could I have dug a shallow well? Did I miss an opportunity? Well, they're moot points now; it's too late.

Amelia covered the magazines with the moist sand and went back to their campsite where she gathered the empty and unusable cans and piled them on top of the sand covering the magazines. She also buried Noonan's map case with his maps, notes and his sextant box with the prized instrument inside. Hopefully, she thought if the Japanese had metal detectors, they would stop digging when they discovered the first layer of items and conclude it was only a garbage dump. Maybe they'd content themselves with the maps and notes. The *Kamoi* came over the horizon as she finished her labor so she used the low bushes for cover as she made her way back to their campsite. Kozaka would regret not keeping an aircraft over the island while he steamed the last 15 miles.

Noonan was awake and babbling incoherently when she returned. Again, she did everything she could to comfort him, but with little success. He was in a world of his own and it wasn't on this island. She managed to get him on his feet and using her body to steady him they both made their way to the beach near the crippled *Electra*.

Kozaka and six members of his crew lowered a life boat from their ship and rowed towards the reef's edge. It was 11:40 local time when Kozaka walked across the practically dry reef to where Amelia and Fred waited. He smiled and bowed slightly and said in perfect English, "Captain Kozaka at your service, Miss Earhart we are glad to find you and Mr. Noonan alive."

JULY 7, 1937

The same day
ONI Headquarters, Washington, D.C.

Lanning was not at all pleased with the way things were going. He sat at his desk glaring at the map on the far wall. He felt a sense of foreboding, something was going wrong, badly wrong; it seemed no one else was aware or cared. This always frustrated him. When he realized that something was amiss, it seemed that he spent too much time trying to convince his superiors that something was wrong. The time could bo better spent on fixing the problem before it got out of hand. In hindsight he could see now that not informing Captain Thompson of the *Itasca* of Earhart's plan to fly to Gardner Island in the event she couldn't locate Howland was a real blunder. Also, his failure to tell Captain Friedell of the *Colorado* to proceed to Gardner with all possible speed only compounded the mistake. Nimitz made those decisions and he had to make the best of them. Everybody in ONI and the White House was hoping that the *Colorado* would find her alive on Gardner, but he couldn't wait for hope. As was his nature, he had to take action. He had Giles send a coded message to Captain Black.

> **TO:** CAPTAIN BLACK
> **FROM:** ORION
> NEED ALL INFORMATION ON COVEY,
> USUAL PAYMENT PLUS EXPRESS
> CHARGE, TIME IS OF THE ESSENCE.

Captain Black was ONI's code name for Kurt G. Feuerstein, the captain of a tramp freighter flying the Swiss flag. He plied the Pacific, mostly the Marshalls, Gilberts, Marianas and Carolinas. He was a con man, black marketer, information conduit and spy for all sides according to how they paid. The Americans, Dutch, English and Australians considered him an intelligence asset. The Japanese liked the black market items he sold and the occasional information he peddled to them. The information the Japanese received was normally given to him for that purpose by one of his other customers. Kurt was a German who worked closely with Richard Sorge, a Nazi newspaper reporter in Tokyo. Feuerstein dealt mostly with Sorge's radioman, Max Claussen. Sorge, code-named "Ramsey", was the premier Soviet spy of the 1930's and 1940's. Feuerstein's Jewish grandmother from Kiev fled to Germany during the pogroms of the late 19th and early 20th centuries. They were his ties with the Soviets, his affinity to communism and virulent hatred of the Cossacks. His Jewish ancestry was the root of his hatred of the Nazis. His love of money and the willingness to take any chance to procure it was a product of his addiction to adrenalin and the ensuing rush it gave him. He was always welcomed no matter where he went in the Pacific. His shallow draft tramp freighter, *Valkyrie*, was the most welcomed ship at all of his many ports-of-call. ONI supplied him with American cigarettes, Cuban cigars, nylons, whiskey and dollars. The Dutch kept him in chocolate, beer, Chinese silk and gilders. The English gave him manufactured mid-level intelligence, cigarettes, Scotch Whiskey, Irish beer (Guinness to be exact) and best of all, pounds sterling. The Aussies kept him in wool, beef and Australian Pounds. Feuerstein carried cargo of rubber from the French in Indochina (Vietnam) and scrap steel from America to the Japanese to help fuel their war machine.

The intelligence he gathered from the Japanese went to the allies; the intelligence given to him by the allies went to the Japanese. It was the best of all possible worlds for the allies and the Japanese, but the Soviets got the straight scoop through Richard Sorge in Tokyo. Feuerstein was the man who would tip off Sorge and the Americans in 1940 of the Japanese plan to attack Pearl Harbor. He also knew that the *Kamoi* was outbound from Kwajalein to the southeast on a secret mission and that it had left on July 3rd. He had ferreted out this information while he had been at Kwajalein on the 4th of July. The Japanese, especially the Tokkeitai officers, craved American cigarettes and Scotch Whiskey (most of them felt that Sake wasn't fit to fuel aircraft). Kurt would cater to these desires, but as was his custom, price and availability would be discussed over several drinks. The Canadian Club was especially popular with the Tokkeitai and he always made sure he brought plenty.

Kurt's generosity meant that only the most eligible young ladies qualified for his attentions in all ports. His insatiable sexual appetite was legendary in the islands. Even though he was in his early forties, his partner preference was a woman between 21 and

24 with a creamy nut brown complexion and long flowing black hair. They had to be ready to please whenever the mood struck him. He was enjoying the favors of one of these prized young beauties in his cabin when the message came from ONI over his radio. "Verdamit noch mal," he swore under his breath. Dammit," changing to English. "What the hell do they want? Don't they know I'm busy?" he asked, as he reluctantly motioned for his latest partner to leave the room. She wrapped her sarong around her near perfect body and left the room not understanding a single word he had said. Kurt listened intently to the Morse code as he copied it on a pad of paper beside the radio. He then took out his code book and deciphered it. He wrote the reply, coded it and then called his soon to be naked island beauty back into the cabin. The island girl adorned with long black hair spilling over her shoulders that tickled her breasts beckoned Kurt. He didn't take the time to answer ONI. They could wait.

Japanese officer, injured Noonan and Amelia on the beach watching the Electra being hoisted aboard the Koshu. Islanders observing staged crash of the Electra.

CHAPTER TWELVE

JULY 8, 1937

Gardner Island, Phoenix Island Group

It was two hours after sunrise and the morning heat was already oppressive. Amelia managed a half-smile through her fear and pain as she met Kozaka's gaze.

"Thank God you found us. Do you have any water? We have had nothing to drink since earlier this morning," she said, forcing herself to appear happy at his presence.

"Of course." He signaled one of his men who produced a canteen from a carrier on his belt. He handed it to Amelia who gave it to Fred. Kozaka motioned for another man to provide an additional canteen to Amelia as he watched Fred sucking on his canteen like a crazed person. She thanked him, resisted the urge to gulp, and took small sips of the tepid water. She savored the moment and enjoyed the elixir like it was fine champagne.

"I will accompany you to your campsite and my men will bring your belongings to the ship. After you, Miss Earhart," he said solicitously.

Amelia knew she needed to appear overjoyed and especially cooperative to this man so he wouldn't suspect she had buried the film on the island. She hoped he would assume that if there were cameras aboard the *Electra* that the canisters were still in place. She led them to the campsite and collected their few belongings, not much to speak of. She hadn't buried Noonan's almanacs because they were easily obtainable and too heavy to carry to the burial site. The sailors took Noonan and her aboard the ship where they were fed a meal of fish, rice and vegetables washed down with some very strong tea. Noonan was taken to the infirmary where a young pharmacist mate tried to ascertain what was wrong with him. When it became apparent to everyone that Noonan's condition was beyond his capabilities, Fred was put in a bunk and made as comfortable as possible. Amelia went out on deck to see what was going on with her aircraft.

The sailors of the *Kamoi* were experienced in sea-plane recovery and were hard at work. The ship was positioned within a hundred yards of the edge of the reef. A rope harness was put in a lifeboat and the end of a crane cable was attached to the back of the boat. The sailors rowed to the reef's edge and hauled the harness and the cable to the plane. Working quickly and efficiently they put the harness around the fuselage and connected the cable. It was mid-afternoon when Kozaka gave the word. The crane began pulling the prize off the reef, which was now covered with 30 inches of water, and then into deep water. Amelia held her breath as her aircraft that had served her so well slid into the water. She hoped it would disappear below the lapping waves. Kozaka knew after his earlier examination that it wouldn't. It would have floated with another 3000 pounds of weight on board. The crane operator skillfully pulled the load to the ship and by 4:25 p.m. local time they had plucked it from the sea and set it on the deck of the *Kamoi*. The sailors lashed it down and covered it with canvas brought from below decks.

Captain Kozaka had opened his sealed orders as the ship steamed northwest from Gardner Island. His commander had told him to go to Gardner Island, secure Earhart and Noonan, put their plane aboard his ship and return to Kwajalein. He was told not to inspect the aircraft and not to openly question either of his "prisoners". Of paramount importance was the need for secrecy. The Japanese Army Secret Police were in no position to let anyone find out they had violated British territory to kidnap two American avia-tors, famous ones, at that! No radio transmissions were to be made regarding Earhart; instead he would make the calls as outlined in the sealed orders.

As Captain Kozaka watched the shore of Gardner Island recede into the distance, he felt confident that his men had gathered all traces of the castaways. He had no way of knowing that Noonan's cigarette lighter and a broken jar of anti-freckle cream lay trampled in the sand. These hidden items would one day bear silent witness to Amelia's and Fred's six day ordeal.

TOP SECRET

JAPANESE INPERIAL NAVY
HEADQUARTERS TOKKEITAI
KWAJALEIN, MARSHALL ISLANDS

TO: CAPTAIN KOZAKA COMMANDER
KAMOI

FROM: CHIEF TOLLEITAI KWAJALEIN
MARSHALL ISLANDS

MISSION: PROCEED TO GARDNER
ISLAND AND RETRIEVE AMELIA
EARHART, HER NAVIGATOR FRED
NOONAN AND THEIR LOCKHEED 10E
ELECTRA AIRCRAFT.
THE FOLLOWING INSTRUCTIONS WILL

BE FOLLOWED TO THE LETTER. UPON ENTERING THE MANDATED ISLANDS YOU WILL MAKE THE FOLLOWING RADIO CALLS ACCORDING TO HOW SUCCESSFUL YOUR MISSION WAS:

IF MISSION WAS SUCCESSFUL REPORT ARRIVING AT ISE BAY ON THE HOME ISLANDS.

IF YOUR MISSION WAS UNSUCESSFUL REPORT EXPECTED ARRIVAL TIME AT KWAJALEIN.

IF YOUR MISSION WAS PARTIALLY SUCCESSFUL REPORT EXPECTED ARRIVAL TIME AT SIAPAN.

WHEN REPORTING ARRIVAL MAKE ALL CALLS ON THE APPROPRIATE RADIO FREQUENCIES FOR YOUR PORT OF ARRIVAL.

DO NOT BYPASS MILI BEFORE MAKING THE ABOVE CALLS.

IMPERATIVE YOU MAKE ALL POSSIBLE SPEED

TOP SECRET

To say Amelia Earhart had mixed emotions is to state the very least. She was physically exhausted; her body had been subjected to tremendous stress during the flight, landing and the subsequent ordeal before their "rescue". Her mental state was almost as bad. Amelia had never dealt with this kind of situation before. She had been out of her element since the landing at Gardner Island. Noonan, whom she had always felt she could count on, had been a burden instead of a help. ONI and the Coast Guard had failed her miserably. They knew the plan. Where the hell were they?

Now she was in the hands of the Japanese Navy and she had no idea what to expect from them, especially when they discovered the cameras aboard the *Electra* and couldn't find the film magazines. Her mind raced from question to question. What would the Japanese do to make me tell them where I had hidden the magazines? Would they take their anger out on Fred if I don't talk? Would they torture us to make us talk? Would the United States Government come to my rescue? Should I confide in Fred? Where was Fred, I hadn't seen him since they took him to sick bay? Was he all right? What is causing me to hurt so badly? These and many other things filled her mind as she fell into a fitful sleep. The coconut crabs resembled large spiders; hungry rats had been replaced with a different, more dangerous group of predators. The situation had morphed from serious to critical; from known dangers to the unknown.

Over the next two days her physical condition improved somewhat. The diet of rice, fish and vegetables were not exactly to her taste, but it was a vast improvement over the tinned beef and condensed milk. She had trouble sleeping because of her constant thoughts about what was going to happen. She had no control over her own destiny and that was a feeling quite foreign to her. Captain Kozaka had been a perfect gentleman and his crew was seemingly very eager to please. No one, as far as she could tell on her daily walks on deck, had bothered to look at the plane. She felt it strange that there were four aircraft on the deck, but her precious flying machine was the only one covered. Alas, she had enough to think about without adding to her woes. Fred was still in sick bay and receiving the best care the pharmacist mate could give him with his limited knowledge of head injuries. Noonan was having severe headaches and was still often delirious, still calling for Marie. He didn't have much of an appetite and was obviously deeply depressed.

JULY 8, 1937

4:00 p.m. EST
ONI Headquarters, Washington, D.C.

The code breakers at ONI were doing everything in their power to crack the latest version of the Japanese Blue code, but there few successes. The pressure from the Bureau of Navigation was increasing by the hour. What was the USS Colorado doing? Had they picked her up yet? What was the *Itasca* doing and where was it? The questions from White House and Nimitz were coming thick and fast, but the answers were few and far between. Lanning didn't know much of anything for sure. The message he had received from Captain Black about the movement of the *Kamoi* really set him on edge. What were the Japs up to? He thought there was no time to plan ahead now, only time to react. A strong-willed, independent man like Lanning despised being in that situation. He knew that the Bureau of

Navigation was under extreme pressure from the White House. Lanning felt he knew the president's predicament, what president wants to be blamed for not rescuing America's sweetheart?

The Navy was already fully involved in the search. The USS *Lexington* was bound for the search area and the USS *Colorado* was on its way to Gardner Island. The people at ONI had no reason to believe that she wouldn't be rescued within the next day or two. Only a certain Lieutenant Commander in the hierarchy of ONI had doubts and those doubts were growing exponentially by the minute.

JULY 9, 1937

Waters off Gardner Island

At 6:56 a.m. the USS *Colorado* launched its three seaplanes to search McKean Island, Gardner Island and Carondelet Reef. The flight was led by Navy Lieutenant J.O. Lambrecht. They searched McKean Island first and quickly decided that Amelia hadn't landed there. It was described as being perfectly flat and only about one square mile in area with a lagoon in the middle which was almost dry. The pilots noted the USS *Colorado* off their starboard side while they were en route from McKean to Gardner Island. At 9:45 a.m. the crew of the Colorado spotted Gardner 15 miles ahead of their course and at 10:20 a.m. they steamed within 11 miles of the island but saw no sign of life. The ship's log noted visibility as being 40 miles at that time. The *Colorado's* aircraft made several circles of the island and saw that there were clearly signs of "recent habitation". But after performing many low passes they saw no signs of life and no answering waves. They had performed their maneuvers at 50 to 100 feet above the surface of the island. The *Colorado's*, crew as well as the aircraft, recorded the presence of the SS *Norwich City*, but nothing else. At 10:35 a.m. the USS *Colorado* hoisted her three seaplanes aboard from a position 16 miles north-east of Gardner Island and left the area secure in the knowledge that Amelia, Fred and the *Electra* were not on Gardner Island.

JULY 10, 1937

The Marshall Island chain

At 11:55 p.m. the *Kamoi* was off the southwest coast of Mili, the most southeasterly island in the Marshall Chain. Captain Kozaka radioed that he was entering Ise Bay, in accordance with his orders. The message reached the chief of the communications section, Lieutenant Commander Ohayashi. He informed his commander within minutes. He couldn't update Sato, the Chief of the Intelligence Section, because he had already departed for Mili Island yesterday.

"Send this to the Kamoi's captain." Ohayashi handed his chief radio operator a message.

TOP SECRET

TO: CAPTAIN KOZAKA

FROM: TOKKEITAI HEADQUARTERS

PROCEED TO MILI LAGOON. LATITUDE
60 DEGREES 04 MINUTES 50 SECONDS

NORTH LONGITUDE 171 DEGREES
44 MINUTES 58 SECONDS EAST. YOU
WILL BE MET BY A FORCE SUFFICIENT
TO CARRY OUT THE MISSION.THE
COMMANDER OF THAT FORCE WILL
BE IN CHARGE OF THE OPERATION.
ARRIVAL MUST BE AT LEAST 2 HOURS
AFTER NIGHT FALL.
SIGNED
COMMANDER TOKKEITAI, KWAJALEIN

TOP SECRET

Captain Kozaka gave the new coordinates to his 1st mate and bent over the chart for the area. They would arrive at the designated location within the hour and he would find out what was really going on at that time.

. . . .

Kozaka and six of his men landed on the ocean side of Mili Island at about one in the morning and he was met by Lieutenant Commander Sato. The *Kamoi* was unable to get into the lagoon at low tide.

"I take it you have the plane on board, sir"

"Yes I do, what is the plan?"

"Unload the plane and we will pull it to a sandbar in the lagoon within 100 feet of the shore. After the aircraft is in place bring Earhart and Noonan ashore and then depart as quickly and quietly as possible. This area has been restricted and the islanders have been kept away from the shores of the lagoon. We must make it appear as though she ditched the aircraft in the lagoon."

"Whose idea was this?"

"Mine,...sir"

"To what end?"

"We have islanders that are working for us who will keep the others in line by telling them what happened. The other residents will come and see the airplane in the lagoon. Two days from now we will arrive with the Geographic survey ship, *Koshu*, which we will say was sent by Tokyo to help the Americans find Earhart. They will hoist the plane onto the ship and take Earhart and Noonan to Kwajalein. It will then appear that she violated our sovereignty and we will appear to have been cooperating when we turn her over to the American authorities."

"Well thought out Sato, I hope it works."

"It will."

The crew of the *Kamoi* joined the contingent of soldiers that had landed with Soto on the island the night before. Jointly they floated the *Electra* to shore, pulled it across the 100 yard wide island, and floated the plane into the lagoon. Finally, they secured it by running it aground on the sandbar about 100 yards from shore.

"What's going on?" Amelia protested as she was awakened and told in broken English to get dressed.

Fred silently obeyed when the sub-lieutenant roused him from his sleep with barely understandable orders.

Both of them were escorted to a makeshift gang-plank and helped into the waiting boat. "Where are you taking us?" Amelia enquired rubbing sleep from her eyes.

"To shore, Miss Earhart, and then we shall depart. I will leave you in the very capable hands of Lieutenant Commander Sato. It has been a pleasant experience for me and I hope for you."

"Thank you for your help. I don't think we would have survived much longer if you hadn't come along."

"My pleasure."

Sato's men helped Amelia and Fred out of the boat and escorted them to shore.

"Good morning, Miss Earhart and Mr. Noonan, welcome to Mili Island. If you would follow me I will show you to your new quarters." He led them along the beach to a grass roofed hut guided by the flash-lights of several of his men. Sato motioned for them to go inside where cots had been set up.

"I hope you will be comfortable. I will see you in 2 days, in the meantime a man and his wife will bring you food tomorrow.

Amelia lay awake all night wondering what was going on. She walked outside at daybreak and caught her breath when she saw the *Electra* aground on a sand bar! The landing gear had been retracted so it looked like she had made a belly landing. Very strange she thought as she started to walk down to the beach. She met a man and his wife on their way to the hut who were carrying a basket of fruit and vegetables and a pot of steaming rice. She and Fred decided to try and enjoy their meal together; relaxing as best as they could under the circumstances.

The next two days were also strange. She and Fred were always followed by the man and woman. Fred and Amelia were never out of their sight, even for a moment. Many people, mostly women and children visited all day long. She couldn't understand what anyone said and they couldn't understand her. The assigned caregivers kept up a steady flow of fruit, vegetables, rice and fish. Fred was feeling a little better.

On the morning of the third day the Japanese

ship, *Koshu*, appeared in the lagoon and without a word began to rig the *Electra* so they could hoist it on board. Sato arrived on a boat from the *Koshu*.

"It's time to leave Miss Earhart. I trust that you haven't been uncomfortable.

"We haven't, the people here have been very nice." She lied as convincingly as she could. In reality, she hadn't been able to sleep since she arrived here and had eaten very little. On the other hand, Fred had gotten over his delirium and was beginning to function a little more normally. However, he still had a long way to go.

JULY 13, 1937

The docks at Kwajalein

Kwajalein was made ready for the clandestine arrival of the most famous female aviator in the world. The *Koshu* docked at 8:37 p.m. the next night and Amelia and Fred were escorted separately off the ship and into two waiting cars. The wharf and headquarters had been cleared of all unnecessary personnel. A naval secret police Commander accompanied them to Tokkeitai Headquarters. They were both greeted by the Commander of the Naval Secret Police

"Good evening, Miss Earhart, I hope you have been made comfortable during your travels."

"Yes admiral, even on Mili Island."

"Yes, well, Lieutenant Commander will see to your needs from now on. Talk to him if you require anything."

It was quite obvious to Amelia that the admiral had been educated in an English school as he had a touch of a British accent. He was, like the British, overly polite and seemingly eager to please, but she sensed that the opposite was true. She sized him up as a ruthless tyrant with people he considered inferior to him.

"Will Mr. Noonan, my navigator be able to get proper medical attention? No one with the proper qualifications has seen him yet."

"By all means." A glance in Sato's direction was all that was necessary.

Amelia doubted this very much but she had felt compelled to ask. She felt it was only a matter of time before they discovered the cameras and then there was going to be hell to pay. The initial meetings were cordial and nondescript. Both the Japanese and Amelia were on their best behavior, each one feigning innocence of the other's motives. That wasn't to last very long. They were both shown to quarters in the compound. Amelia was in a hut that was divided in half and obviously for use by a woman. Noonan was put in a small room near the prison compound, where he could hear the screams of the people being interrogated.

Within an hour the *Electra* was being inspected by four aviation experts, two mechanics and two pilots. It was scrutinized more closely than it had been since it had left the Lockheed plant in Burbank, California. It was 3:30 in the morning when they gave their report to Headquarters that the plane was equipped with a Fairchild F-24 aerial camera under the navigator's station in the rear fuselage and two Leica Reporter Cameras, one in each wing. The cameras were hidden by doors flush with the aircraft skin and operated by what were probably automobile windshield wiper motors. The wing cameras were operated by a switch, under the pilot's seat. The F-24 under the navigator's station was operated by a switch just under the edge of the table top. None of the cameras had any film in them. It didn't appear to the team that anything else was out of the ordinary except there were no maps, sextant or navigator's notes to be found.

Lieutenant Commander Sato's insides churned as he listened to the measured, stern formal words of his Commander, Japanese Imperial Navy Rear Admiral Nakashima.

"Miss Earhart has photographed our secret base at Truk Atoll, there is no doubt! Her aircraft is proof that she was spying. The film is missing from the cameras and you will consult with Commander Kichida for details of what the team found or rather didn't find. We must and I emphasize the word must find those films. That is your job; she must be made to tell us where the films are. My career is on the line, but you have much more to lose DO...I...make...myself... clear?" He enunciated His black eyes flashed as raised his voice slightly.

"Yes, sir!" came Sato's clipped reply. He spun on his heels and left the office. He knew quite well what Nakashima meant. Just last week 3 sailors and a petty officer had been executed for failing to follow orders and orders were what Sato had just received. He went immediately to Kichida's office and requested the full report on what had been found on the Earhart plane. He took the copy with him. It was 6 a.m. when he returned to his office and the gloves were about to come off.

July 9, 1937 picture of Gardner Island taken by a pilot of a plane from the USS Colorado.

CHAPTER THIRTEEN

JULY 14, 1937

Intelligence Section Interrogation Building

"Get Earhart and Noonan to Interrogation rooms A and D and let me know when they're there." He spoke the orders in a quiet, menacing manner to the young sub-lieutenant, Yamato, who was assigned as his assistant. The young man clicked his heels in reply and quickly left the room. Sub-lieutenant Yamato knocked on Amelia's door and she appeared a minute later with what she hoped was her usual smile. Yamato motioned for her to follow him down the hall and she complied. An armed guard silently fell in step behind them. He ushered her into a room with bare walls and only furnished with a single wooden chair in the center of the room. She sat down when the young sub-lieutenant indicated she should sit. Noonan was treated with less formality. He was held between two guards and more or less dragged to room D where he was unceremoniously seated by the two rather large sailors. When he tried to get up the sub lieutenant hit him across the shoulders with a bamboo rod that he had picked up when he entered the room. Noonan groaned as he fell back onto into the chair. Goddamn that son-of-a-bitch, if I could just get that blasted rod away from him, I'd beat his head into mush. Just wishful thinking, of course, as Fred knew that wouldn't happen. The young sub-lieutenant had 20 years on him and wasn't in constant pain.

Amelia rose when Sato entered the room. He frowned and said, "Sit down, Miss Earhart."

"I prefer to stand, if you don't mind," displaying no emotion, forcing her face to be impassive.

Sato placed his riding crop on her shoulder and pressed down as he said, "Your preferences are no longer our concern. We have proof that you are an American spy, a capital offense both in Japan and your country. You will cooperate with us if you and Mr. Noonan wish to live. Am I understood?"

"Yes." came her unruffled reply. Although she had a firm grip on her expression and voice, inside she was trembling with trepidation. She smiled slightly as she realized that he had forced her to sit because at five foot seven she was a little taller than he was.

"We have inspected your plane and found the

cameras and we know that you flew over our civilian base at Truk Atoll. We want the film that you took and when we get it we will return you to the American authorities. Otherwise, you will be tried for espionage and executed or imprisoned for life. It is your choice."

"I don't know anything about cameras on my aircraft. It was rebuilt at Lockheed in Burbank and I wasn't permitted to inspect it until it was ready to be test flown. They said they had made modifications to the structure to make it safer. That's all I know, perhaps Purdue University had cameras installed for some future project they had in mind. I'm not aware of the presence of cameras, so how would I know about film?" Her demeanor was a little haughty towards the last of her speech.

"Have it your way, we will see if you are telling the truth!" Sato had begun tapping the riding crop against his leg trying not to show his nervousness at her denial. He left the room and went directly to Room D where the unsuspecting Noonan sat.

"Noonan, your companion doesn't seem to want to cooperate with me. Possibly you will be more cautious about your dilemma. Where is the film?" he asked through clenched teeth, his red face betraying his cool demeanor.

"Do you know where Maria is? When are they coming to get us? They're supposed to......they said they would." Sato backhanded Noonan and nodded to the guard behind Noonan as he turned and left the room. Noonan yelped in pain, his lip began to bleed. He cried out again as the guard brought the bamboo rod down on his shoulder. Fred was suddenly and very acutely aware of what was going on. What do they want to know? Why did he just bash me in the face? That squinty eyed little bastard wouldn't have the guts to do that man to man, without his buddy behind me. Fred maintained his façade of mental confusion, hoping it would make him less likely to be tortured.

"What the hell do you want?—Tell me what you want!" cried Noonan through his pain and anger. The guard stepped back because he didn't speak English and had no idea what Noonan had said. Sato reentered the room and jerked his head towards the door and the guard quickly left.

"We want to know where the film is!" Sato demanded.

"I don't know!" Noonan's voice was angry. He let out another painful yelp and then blacked out when Sato struck him on his head wound with his riding crop.

Amelia heard it all because the doors to both rooms were open. She cringed when she heard Noonan's yelp immediately after the crack of the crop had landed on his injured head. She knew that they would continue to work on them both until she told them where the films were, but she gritted her teeth and promised herself that she would cling to her story, no matter what happened!

She felt a certain sense of relief when she was jerked from the chair by two guards and practically dragged across the sparse compound towards a wooden building with four doors and no windows. Another guard opened one of the doors and she was thrown unceremoniously into the six-foot-by-eight-foot cell. A few minutes later she heard Noonan moan as he was thrown into a cell at the other end of the building. The tiny room must have been a hundred and ten degrees. The heat, combined with high humidity and her fear caused sweat to pour off her in rivers even though she hardly moved a muscle. The room cooled down about 10 degrees when darkness fell. She had been in the cell about 3 hours when a small flap opened at the base of the door and a plate of cold rice and a cup of foul smelling liquid suddenly appeared. The "broth" tasted awful, but she drank it anyway. It did nothing to quench her thirst. She slept on and off for a few hours until the door flew open and the same two guards stepped in, jerked her to her feet and dragged her to another building behind the row of cells.

Sato had realized that Noonan's pain wasn't going to do much to loosen Earhart's tongue. Amelia would never give him the information if he tortured them too brutally, because she would conclude that he wouldn't release them. He knew that the torture itself was useless; it was the fear of brutality that would loosen tongues. Therefore, he decided to use fear to erode her resolve. When she was forced into the room, he stood up from his chair, smiled and quickly, but quietly asked, "Have you decided to tell us the location of the film?"

"I don't know about any film!" she protested. Her eyes were focused on the water-filled bathtub beside Sato's chair. He nodded his head and one of the guards looped a rope around one wrist and forcefully yanked her arm behind her back. He then grabbed the other wrist and roughly tied her hands. The ropes immediately began to burn into her flesh and started to cut off the circulation to her hands.

"One last chance. Don't make this any harder

than it has to be." There was no sympathy in his voice.

"I don't know what you are talking about!" she protested.

Sato nodded and the guards dragged her to the edge of the bathtub and forced her to her knees. She struggled, but one of them grabbed her hair, pushed her head under the water and held it there. She held her breath until she thought her lungs would burst and then began to slowly exhale. Her chest was throbbing as she fought the overwhelming desire to inhale. The guard pulled her head out of the water and she inhaled, choking on the water that was sucked into her lungs along with the much welcomed air.

"Where are the films?" His voice was low, measured and menacing.

Her scalp burned from the guard's grip, but she just stared at him and panted. He nodded and once again her head was thrust back into the water. She concentrated on the pain in her knees and wrists to take her mind off the driving desire to breathe. Each time her head was brought out of the water he would ask the same question in the same tone and she would defiantly resist his efforts. They repeated the dance over and over and over: the predator and prey. This went on for what seemed like hours before she was dragged to the cell and her wrists untied. Amelia noticed the first rays of sun over the shoulders of the guards in the doorway as it slammed shut, leaving her in almost total darkness.

The Japanese sailors made their way to Noonan's cell and she knew that he was in for the same torture. She felt totally helpless to help him or herself. When would the American cavalry come riding over the hill to rescue her from this hell, just like they always did in the movies? She prayed it would be soon.

After two days of concentrated questioning Sato worried that he was about out of methods to loosen their tongues. Normally, dunking produced the desired results. He had hung them by their feet for hours on end. Sato would suddenly release the rope and they would go crashing to the dirt floor. Their faces and heads got bloodied and bruised each time, because their arms were useless to cushion the fall. Hanging upside-down had made the blood pool in their arms and they would buckle on impact. Noonan had been beaten with a length of rubber hose while Earhart looked on. They hadn't been fed more than two handfuls of rice and 2 cups of bitter tea a day. Nothing had worked. He couldn't start pulling out fingernails or cutting off fingers and toes as they couldn't possibly return her to the Americans mutilated! Amelia finally cracked on the morning of July 16th when she was bound hand and foot and placed in a room with cages of rats, driven mad with hunger and thirst.

Sato had said, "Do you need to imagine how horrible your death will be after I have the cages opened?"

"Go ahead, do it, kill me you little bastard, explain that to the world. I would sooner die than tell you anything, even if I knew it......KILL US, GODDAMMIT, KILL US BOTH, YOU SON-OF-A-BITCH!" she screamed, her face red and veins popping out on her forehead. He was taken aback at the ferocity of her tirade, expecting that she had reached the end of her rope. He nodded at the guards and they took her back to her cell. Sato had lost and he knew it. He had done all he could. He cringed as he reported his failure to his commander. Rear Admiral Nakashima gave orders for the two to be cleaned-up and readied for transport to Saipan: This was headquarters' problem now.

JULY 9, 1937

ONI Headquarters, Washington, D.C.

Lanning sat stunned after reading the message in his hand. The USS *Colorado* hadn't found any trace of Earhart, Noonan or the *Electra* on Gardner Island. He rubbed his head as he tried to think of what could have happened.

He queried Captain Black again and promised to double his usual fee for any information. Black had seen an opportunity to soak ONI for a bundle of cash. He steamed back to Kwajalein to gather as much information as he could. He knew that he would squeeze ONI for three times his fee when he finally got the information they wanted. Black contacted Tokyo for help to see what they knew. Sorge was quick to reply that they had no knowledge of Earhart's whereabouts, although they would look into it.

"Our asses, all of our asses are hanging out on this one!" Lanning said to his office desk as he banged his fist down. He would get no sleep that night wondering what they could do to salvage something from this gargantuan screw up. He would lose sleep, but Amelia would not sleep more than an hour at a time for the next few months. Fred Noonan would be in agony and sleep was out of the question. Amelia and Fred were now in the process of learning an old military axiom. "Decisions made by your superiors seldom, if ever, have your best interests at heart."

*"A good plan violently executed now is better
than a perfect plan executed next week."*
— *General George S. Patton Jr.*

CHAPTER FOURTEEN

JULY 15, 1937

The *Kamoi* left Kwajalein on July 15th bound for the Naval Headquarters at Tanapag Seaplane Base, Saipan. Captain Kozaka carried on normal radio operations. At the Pan Am DF stations on Midway, Wake and Hawaii the radio calls from the *Kamoi* were located and tracked. Although the operators recorded the messages in the uncracked Blue code enough is known to ascertain that the ship was the *Kamoi*. Jim Jarvis, a radio operator on Wake, noticed that the ship docked at Kwajalein the 11th of July, but something was wrong. He searched his records and contacted the other two DF stations for information on the *Kamoi* from June 30th to July 11th. Both of the stations had the same observations he had. He voiced his concerns to his supervisor.

"The *Kamoi* was docked at Kwajalein on the 30th of June and we had tracked her progress as she cruised in the Carolinas and Marianas with the *Okinashima*, *Asanagi* and *Yunagi*. They all docked at Kwajalein on the 29th and 30th of June. I show normal radio traffic at Kwajalein for all three ships but nothing from the *Kamoi*. The *Kamoi* seems to have been very quiet from July 2nd until the 10th when we picked up a call from her in the Blue code. She was cruising in the vicinity of Mili Island, in the southern Marshalls, and docked at Kwajalein on July 11th. As far as we can tell she was running in total radio silence from the 3rd through the 10th of July until it appeared in the southern Marshalls. It seems quite strange to me."

"Hmmm, you may have something here. Let me see the intercepts."

Jarvis' supervisor, Lane Willingham, had a soft spoken manner that belied the razor sharp mind behind his placid face. He took the intercepts from Jarvis and looked them over briefly.

Good work, Jim, it seems strange to me too. Send a report to station Baker on Guam and let them decide how important it is."

"Will do Lane!"

By the morning of July 17th the message from Station Baker was on Lanning's desk. He knew that intelligence was gleaned from all the things you saw and heard, but more often than not, it also came from things you expected to hear or see and didn't. This report was earth shattering when it was coupled with Captain Black's intelligence. Knowing that Amelia had planned to go to Gardner Island in the event that she couldn't find Howland, along with the facts that she wasn't there and that searchers found signs of recent habitation led him to a very disturbing conclusion. A line drawn from Kwajalein to the point provided by the Pan Am DF operators and continued south led, suspiciously, to the vicinity of Gardner Island. It was not conclusive, but it was definitive enough for him to call Giles to send a message.

TOP SECRET

EYES ONLY: ASSISTANT CHIEF BUREAU OF NAVIGATION
STRONG EVIDENCE POINTS TO THE JAPANESE BEING THE REASON COVEY WASN'T FOUND ON GARDNER ISLAND. I WILL CONTINUE TO INVESTIGATE THIS AVENUE
L

There was no reply, none was expected. Knowing that Amelia, Noonan and their aircraft had been captured was not enough to prompt the State Department and the President to do anything about it. This decision to do nothing was because of the current political climate between the U.S. and the Axis Power Alliance. The official search for Amelia Earhart was concluded on the 19th of July at 4:20 local time in the search area. The *Electra* and its occupants were officially lost at sea. It cost the federal government just over sixty millions of today's dollars to come up empty-handed.

On the afternoon of July 20th the *Kamoi* arrived at the seaplane base north of Garapan on the island of Saipan. The *Electra* was unloaded onto the quay and towed into a hanger at the southeast corner of the base. It was covered as it had been on the deck of the *Kamoi* and listed in the official record as evidence. It was restricted from further scrutiny and preserved to back-up Japanese allegations of espionage against Earhart and Noonan. The order was signed by Vice Admiral Hashimoto commander of the Tokkeitai Pacific Region. No one dared disturb it without his signed consent.

JULY 21, 1937

Kwajalein Airfield, Kwajalein Atoll

Amelia and Fred were taken aboard a Mitsubishi G3M Medium Bomber that had been dispatched from Saipan to transport them to Tokkeitai Headquarters Pacific at Garapan, Saipan. The dispatch had been written to pick up VIPs for return to Saipan. The Japanese were taking no chances that they would be accused of kidnapping the famous aviatrix and her navigator. The pair walked to the plane under their own power, dressed in worn khaki flying clothes borrowed from the supply room at the airport. It was obvious on close observation that both were suffering from pain and stress. Fred walked like a man dazed, shielding his eyes from the rising tropical sun. Amelia stepped carefully and her eyes were on the ground. There were outward signs of physical torture on them both, mainly bruises, and they both definitely showed the signs of extreme mental exhaustion. Noonan's head was extensively bandaged and he complained of a constant pounding headache. Amelia looked pale, thinner and had lost the desire and possibly the ability to smile.

Rear Admiral Nakashima had been very careful to not allow anyone except his naval secret police personnel know about the presence of the famous pair. The men of the Tokkeitai were specially chosen for their devotion to duty and ability to carry out orders normally distasteful to ordinary soldiers. Amelia had not cracked under pressure to reveal the location of the film magazines and Noonan didn't know. Lieutenant Commander Sato was in disgrace because of her refusal to talk. He would not be executed, but he had seen his last promotion and soon was transferred from the intelligence section to the enforcement branch. He would be instrumental in the murder of 150 American prisoners-of-war on the island of Palawan in the Philippines. He would be killed by the Lieutenant Colonel Henry Mucci's 6th Ranger Battalion during the raid on Cabanatuan on the evening of January 30, 1945.

They arrived at Truk Atoll at a little after 11 o'clock in the morning after an eventful five-and- a -half hour flight. The left engine had begun to run rough about 50 miles out. Amelia felt exhilarated at being in the air once again, in spite of the engine trouble. The Mitsubishi landed at the partially completed airport and taxied to the refueling area near the unfinished Lufthansa hangar. They were taken off the transport so it could be refueled and repaired for the trip to Saipan. Amelia and Fred were shaky and looked like they were on their last legs when the guard motioned them towards a small guard shack about 350 feet away.

As the aircraft was being refueled, several mechanics were pulling the cowling off the left engine. Amelia watched intently as one of the mechanics ran to another hangar next to the Lufthansa hangar. Within the hour another guard appeared and they motioned for the pair to get up and come with them. They walked slowly to the adjacent hangar and were pushed into a storeroom that was locked behind them. Hours later a guard brought them some cold rice and water. They both were allowed to go to the bathroom and then locked up again. Amelia and Fred did their best to be comfortable on a pile of rags in the corner and tried to sleep.

Before 6 o'clock the next morning they were prodded awake by a guard's rifle butt and ushered outside. The sun was just coming up as they walked towards the Lufthansa hangar where the *Iron Annie*, a Lufthansa JU-52 airliner, was idling on the taxiway not far from where the Mitsubishi was being readied to start its engines. Amelia nudged Fred when she noticed the pilot get out of the German airliner and walk towards the hangar. Their guard was not paying much attention to them, seemingly more interested in grabbing a cigarette. His rifle was slung over his shoulder and his hands were in his pocket searching for a match. Fred raised his eyebrows when Amelia nodded towards the running aircraft. They both casually walked the 30 feet to the open door, trying to look as curious as possible.

The guard was just getting his cigarette lit when Amelia slipped through the open door and bolted towards the cockpit. Fred suddenly sensed possible freedom and felt an unbelievable adrenaline rush that over-shadowed his pain. Shrewdly, he watched the guard until he heard the engines begin to increase RPM's. Using his last bit of strength he jumped into the open door and closed it behind him as the plane lurched forward. The guard's mouth dropped open and the cigarette hit the tarmac about the time he unslung his rifle. Noonan locked the door and hugged the floor as the guard began to empty his rifle into the side of the corrugated metal body of the aircraft. The engines strained as Amelia rammed the throttles to full open. The aircraft jumped forward over the wheel chocks and seconds later lifted into the air just before Amelia ran out of taxiway. The JU-52 banked hard left as she turned south towards Lae, New Guinea.

"Give me a heading......Quick!" She yelled generally towards the back of the aircraft.

"Northwest, try three- two- five degrees to start with and I'll get you a better one in a minute," Fred shouted over the engine noise as he climbed into the co-pilots seat, grabbing a chart on the way.

Amelia turned to a heading of 325 degrees and leveled off at a hundred feet above the waves.

"How are we on gas?" he asked as he unfolded the chart.

'The gauges indicate full. Where should we go?"

"Guam is our only chance. If I remember, it's less than 700 miles from Truk to Guam. Can this bucket make it?"

"It should, like you said, it's our only chance. I'm sure the Japs were not going to let us go. I doubt that anybody on our side is coming after us, so it looks like we're on our own." She stated this matter-of-factly, without emotion as she leaned the mixture to the engines to the point of them stalling. Amelia knew their luck had to hold out or they would both be dead shortly.

The Japanese reacted instantly and the one flyable fighter left on the island was soon airborne, piloted by Lieutenant Goto. He swept the skies around Truk Atoll for ten minutes and then began his search in a southerly direction. Goto spent a half an hour searching towards Lae and then turned north back towards Truk. Goto's many years of experience made him very adept at scrutinizing the ocean. He had climbed to 8,000 feet and his eyes scanned the waves below. Scattered clouds at 2000 feet made his search extremely difficult since they cast shadows on the ocean and he had the disadvantage of looking for a silver aircraft on an ocean reflecting the sunlight back at him. Several times he thought he spotted the JU-52, affectionately known as *Iron Annie*, only to realize it was an optical illusion. Where the hell could they have gone? Would they have tried to make it to Guam? Goto was puzzled as he reasoned that they don't have enough fuel to make it to Guam. His plane could easily outperform the airliner but, nevertheless, it had eluded him. Who was this woman? Was she in league with the devil? He searched for the next 3 hours before he was forced to return to Truk empty handed. The Americans had eluded him once again and he was very unhappy about it.

Noonan had no way of telling what their ground speed was or if they were on course. He used the map and the position of the sun to estimate their position, but he had no chronometers because the aircraft only flew between the islands in Truk Atoll. The pilots had no use for fancy navigational instruments, just an old crumpled up chart that looked like a wadded-up newspaper. He was navigating from memory: reliving his time flying to Truk two weeks ago, his knowledge of Guam from his extensive experience flying with Pan Am and setting up the Clipper Routes for their scheduled flights. Noonan knew he could get close, but gauging the wind would be the problem since he had no way of telling which way it was blowing except from the waves below. He guessed they had a 10 to 15 mile per hour tail wind. He was almost right except it was blowing off their left rear taking them north of his intended course.

JULY 20, 1937

The same day
Kwajalein Atoll, North Pacific Ocean

Kurt Feuerstein sailed into Kwajalein about an hour after Amelia had stolen the Lufthansa JU-52 at Truk. He set to work immediately gathering information as best he could. He had little success, nobody was talking. Everybody was afraid they might be linked with Sato's failure if they even mentioned Amelia Earhart or Fred Noonan. There were rumors among the senior officers that an American woman was a prisoner over at the Tokkeitai compound. Kurt's contacts were not very keen on talking about the doings of the secret police. They were especially uncomfortable with speculating on what the secret police did in their own compound. Kurt hung out all that evening until two in the morning listening to scuttlebutt among the sailors at the various bars. He gathered that two Europeans or Americans, a white man and woman, had indeed been there for several days, but had left early this morning. The general feeling was they weren't going to last very long if they didn't cooperate. He contacted ONI at about 2 a.m. with what he had gathered. Kurt had chosen a "belly warmer" from among the girls at the different bars who were more than happy to accompany him to his next port. No need to suffer from loneliness he thought. The girls all knew that they could ply their trade in the Gilberts better than here in the Marshalls: a few nights under Kurt was an enjoyable price. Kurt was assured by the Man from ONI that his shipment of cigarettes, nylons and Canadian Club would be ready in the Gilberts when he arrived, along with a fat wad of US dollars.

JULY 20, 1937

1 hour after the Lufthansa theft
Truk Airport, Truk Atoll

Josef Schmidt, the head of the Lufthansa operation on Truk Atoll, was angrier than anybody had ever seen him. He had chewed out his co-pilot for leaving the aircraft running while he went to get a cup of coffee.

"Schiesekopt, what the hell is wrong with you, leaving the aircraft running with no one at the controls? I distinctly told you to warm it up while I got the weather report."

"Herr Schmidt, the wheels were chocked, I was certain it would be in ordnung to let it warm up, while I went back into the hangar."

"Well we are both in trouble now. You are in deep shit with me and I am in deeper shit with Lufthansa and the Luftwaffe. Who do you think owned that airplane? This is our foothold in the mandated islands and now because of your stupidity...never mind... get out of my sight while I think."

"But Herr…"

"ROUSE OUT, OUT, NOW!!!"

The young pilot, who would be an ace in the Luftwaffe 10 times over before his death at the hands of a P-51 pilot in 1944, left the hangar while Schmidt tried to telephone his superiors in Tokyo. Lufthansa was very busy since the war with China had begun on the 7th of July. They, like the company building the installations on Truk, were civilian in name only. Schmidt was a Major in the Luftwaffe. The "workers" building the hangars, wharfs, airfields were Japanese soldiers and sailors. This was a huge operation and now it was in jeopardy of being uncovered.

Rear Admiral Nakashima, commander of the secret police at Kwajalein, smiled as he read the radio report detailing the theft of the Lufthansa airliner on Truk. His commanders, on Saipan, would be so involved with finding Earhart and Noonan they would forget that he hadn't been able to extract any information from her about the whereabouts of the film. The report stated that the navy had failed in its mission to transport two unarmed prisoners from Kwajalein to Saipan. They, the navy, had been so lax in its security that two unarmed prisoners had stolen an aircraft of a foreign power and flown to who-knows-where. Nakashima knew that a full investigation would ensue. The Tokkeitai would do the digging and then they would write the report absolving themselves, including him, from any dereliction of duty. The sailor guarding them would be executed as an example. Sato's fall from grace would spur the other officers of the Tokkeitai to do as they were told, period. Everything was going to turn out all right. All available aircraft from Saipan, limited due to the war in China, were patrolling around the American possession of Guam. They had orders to shoot down the JU-52 so it couldn't land at Guam. Earhart and Noonan didn't stand a chance, so he poured himself a shot of Kurt's Canadian Club to savor the moment. He opened his desk drawer to reveal two pairs of nylons that he would give his latest "friend" tonight before they celebrated. He knew that Kurt (Captain Black) was selling any information that he gathered, but he was a necessary evil to make life in these forsaken islands livable.

JULY 20, 1937

Mariana Islands, Pacific Ocean

It was 11:30 a.m. when Amelia saw the hint of land off

the nose of her *Iron Annie*, which she had found very sluggish on the controls but easy to fly. It seemed to want to fly without being coaxed. It wasn't her beloved, faithful friend, the *Electra,* but it provided a path to freedom. Noonan stared intently at the approaching land and declared, "It could be Guam, I can't tell from this altitude. Can we go higher?"

"Probably to a thousand feet, I don't want to go much higher for fear of being spotted." She pulled back on the yoke and began a gentle climb to a thousand feet. After she leveled off, she shut down the center engine: there were three. She feathered the prop to cut down resistance, hoping to conserve fuel. The gauges were bumping "empty" much too often for her comfort.

"Shoot for the northern third of the island. The harbor and airfield are on the west side, so they should be to your left when we go over the ridge line in the middle of the island."

"Will do," she concurred as she turned ever so slightly to the right to avoid the higher mountains to the south."

"The runway parallels the beach and we should pick it up as soon as we cross the mountains."

Amelia simply nodded her head as she had more important things going on just now: two of the three fuel gages had stopped moving and were pointing to empty and the third one wasn't far behind. "It looks like we may have just made it if the fuel lasts another couple of minutes." Her apprehension didn't show through in her voice.

They were about a mile off shore when Noonan exclaimed, "Oh my God!"

"What's wrong?" Her voice was surprised.

"I don't think this is Guam, the mountains on Guam are only three to four hundred feet high, and those to the south are over a thousand feet. I think this might be Rota or possibly Saipan!"

"It doesn't make any difference now; we don't have the fuel to go anyplace else!"

At that moment the left engine sputtered. Amelia jammed the mixture lever to "full rich" and it smoothed out for about 20 seconds, and then quit. She feathered the prop and glanced at Fred as she calmly stated, "Hang on and hope the airport is over that ridge ahead." The right engine sputtered and seconds later quit altogether. She pulled the nose slightly up to get the maximum glide speed. Noonan tightened his seat belt.

Hotel Kobayashi-Royokan Garapan, Saipan.

CHAPTER FIFTEEN

JULY 20, 1937

Saipan, Mariana Islands

Josephine Blanco, a Chamorro native, was bicycling towards the Japanese Chico base where her brother-in-law, J.Y. Matsumoto, worked as a construction laborer. She was taking him his lunch, as she did every day around noon, when she heard an aircraft engine behind her and then silence. She looked over her shoulder and saw a silver colored airplane coming over the ridge line and descending towards her. Josephine stood frozen in place as the aircraft clipped the tops of the trees between her and the base. Seconds later she heard it impact the ground.

Her brother-in-law, standing in the shade of the trees, ducked as the aircraft took out the tops of the trees above him. He stared in horror as the aircraft hit the sand, the wheels dug in and the landing gear collapsed. He had covered his head and fallen to the ground to avoid being hit by falling branches. Then he peeked out from under his arms and watched one of the pilots stumble out of the plane, apparently injured, stagger several feet from the wrecked plane and collapse to the ground. The other pilot got out and started towards the man on the ground. Japanese soldiers, several officers among them, were already on the scene and they pushed the second pilot away from the one on the ground. They kept the civilians away from the scene and tried to subdue the pilots. The one lying face down on the sand (Noonan) was trying to move. The other pilot (Amelia) pulled away from the soldier trying to restrain her and ran towards Noonan. She was knocked to the ground with the butt of a rifle and lay stunned. Noonan rolled over and tried to get up, but he gave up the idea when a soldier placed a bayonet at his throat.

One of the officers ordered several soldiers to strip the pilots. Amelia and Fred both protested violently in English to no avail. The soldiers stripped off their shirts and stopped short when it became apparent from Amelia's undergarments that she was a woman. Thomas Blas, a construction worker very close to the scene, remembered many years later that the soldiers and officers alike were embarrassed by the discovery and quickly re-dressed them. The Japanese soldiers were laughing and bantered nervously.

"The Americans must be running out of pilots because they are using women to fly their airplanes."

"What kind of man would let a woman fly while he just rode along?"

Fred went back into his delirious act and felt rather badly that Amelia couldn't do the same. The soldiers blindfolded both Amelia and Fred, but didn't tie them up. They loaded them like cargo into a waiting car and drove off towards Garapan. The officers and soldiers told all the Saipanese natives to go home, because work was over for the day. A man with a camera arrived and began taking pictures of the wreck as the workers left the scene.

Amelia and Fred were driven to the Hotel Kobayashi-Royokan in east Garapan village. The hotel was being operated a kind of a prison by the Japanese. The hotel was not much different than the prison except it was a bit more civilized. They were taken separately to the Headquarters of the Tokkeitai the next morning to be questioned by a Major Toyota, possibly a relative of the famous Admiral of WWII fame. His questions were very general because he didn't have full knowledge of Sato's interrogation. However, he was quite explicit about what would happen to them if they refused to cooperate.

"Believe me, you will be very sorry if you don't give me the information I seek. We have a Saipanese native who is very adept at extracting information from, shall we say, uncooperative individuals. His name is Jesus, very ironic, yes?" He smiled at his little joke as Amelia just looked at him said nothing. It would have been pointless to provoke him, anyway.

"You don't seem very well, is there anything I can have brought to you? Life will get much better if you just cooperate. We are not barbarians you know." Again, Amelia just looked at him and said nothing.

"Have it your way, we will see how you feel in a few days. I'm sure that the crash has affected you. Maybe you need more time to think about what I have said. His smile was patronizing and full of malice.

Noonan got the same speech and his response was much the same. He and Amelia both knew that they had little or no chance of survival now. Her mission to fly around the world was a failure. There was only one way for the mission to succeed: The U.S. Navy could still recover the film magazines from its hiding place on Gardner Island, that is, only if she could prevent the Japanese from learning the film's location. She was now willing to sacrifice everything to insure that outcome; her only hope is that their sacrifice wouldn't be in vain.

By the middle of August they had been questioned several times by Major Toyota. The diet of rice and tea was not conducive to their good health. The victims were exhibiting symptoms of dysentery and malnutrition. Their days at the hotel were numbered. Amelia spent less and less time outside and more time in her bed or running to the outhouse. Fred was also in the hotel and was not in much better shape. In the hopes of loosening her tongue the Japanese allowed Amelia and Fred to roam the hotel and its limited grounds freely. Fred chose to stay in his room except for meals, but he ate less and less and his trips to the outhouse became more frequent. Amelia was invited to Mrs. Matilda Aniola Saint Nicholas's house next to the hotel. The Japanese guards didn't object because they were sure she wasn't going to try to get away: after all, they were on an island. Mrs. Saint Nicholas was very sympathetic. Mrs. Saint Nicholas later remarked to her younger sister the next day, "She seemed so pale and sickly looking, I don't think the Japanese are treating her very well." As was the custom on the island Mrs. Saint Nicholas offered food, but Amelia ate only a few bites of fruit. In another conversation she again confided to her sister. With a great deal of compassion and pity in her voice, she said, "We parted on a friendly note even though she seemed very preoccupied. She had a very distant look in her eyes and I am sure she was in pain and getting sick."

The unfortunates underwent their first interrogation by Jesus De Leon Guerrero, alias, "Kumoi", the chief investigator for the Japanese police on Saipan. The Japanese at the Garapan prison were accustomed to the screams emitting from Guerrero's "interrogations." Amelia's encounter wasn't any different. Guerrero enjoyed crushing out cigarettes on his victim's neck and the side of the face. He was especially adept at the application of a blow torch to the arms. He was an absolute master at this, because he knew when to stop: when he produced first and second degree burns! He knew third degree burns destroy the nerves and the victim feels no pain.

Later on in the week Amelia revisited Mrs. Saint Nicholas and her sister. The right side of her face and neck were full of burns and bruises and her left forearm was bandaged. She was obviously in a great deal of pain and very pale. Mrs. Saint Nicholas saw the obvious signs of abuse, but knew it was not her place to comment on it. Amelia managed a weak smile when she was offered food and simply shook her head, no. Every time she ate it meant another trip to the outhouse, which she found especially repugnant.

"What is your sister working on?" Amelia inquired.

"Her homework from school." Mrs. Saint Nicholas's smile was genuine. She was quite touched that a person in such distress would take an interest in what the young girl was working on. Amelia looked over her shoulder and asked," What are you working on, dear?"

"It's my geography lesson. I'm trying to correctly place the Marianas where they belong with the other islands in the Pacific

"I think if you put Saipan here. It will all work out for you."

"That does look better, and then Guam goes here." She pointed to Guam's correct location.

"Yes, you are very correct, young lady,"

Again Amelia left on a friendly note. She had enjoyed the interlude and Mrs. Saint Nicholas would never forget her.

Three days later they were unobtrusively snatched from the hotel, bound and blindfolded, and driven away in an open vehicle. Mrs. Saint Nicholas talked to a busboy acquaintance who worked at the hotel about a week after they were taken away.

The bus boy told her, "I saw her bed the day before she left and it was soaked with blood. I think she was very sick." Mrs. Saint Nicholas shook her head and muttered under her breath upon being told of the fate of "Tokyo Rosa" (as Amelia was popularly called by the natives). She never saw Amelia Earhart again.

AUGUST 7, 1937

ONI Headquarters, Washington, D.C.

It was a typical summer day in Washington D.C. It had dawned hot and hazy. Lanning arrived at his office at 6 a.m. sharp as was his custom. There were no messages on his desk from the night before and he was looking forward to another job now that the Earhart matter was beginning to die down a little bit. The general public was still demanding more than the bits and pieces they were being fed. The official report was still being worked on, but leaks to key members of the press were starting to work in ONI's favor. The story was simply that she had disappeared while trying to find Howland Island. The government had spent over four million dollars and tied up a battleship, aircraft carrier, coast guard cutter and numerous smaller ships to conduct the search of 150,000 square miles of the vast Pacific Ocean. They had found nothing.

ONI had leaked several stories, unofficial of course: "She had panicked and spun her aircraft into the deep blue." "She had simply gotten lost, run out of gas and sunk below the waves." Not surprisingly, the reports of radio calls after she disappeared were all debunked as "a fabrication by sick individuals bent on God knows what." All these stories clouded the issue and added to the confusion. There were individuals who believed she had been picked up by the Japanese, but they were quickly discounted by the "experts". Things weren't going as smoothly as everyone would have liked, but all was going as well as could be expected.

George Putnam, Amelia's husband, had financed a private search of the area near Howland and the Gilbert Islands. In late July he had commissioned two boats to conduct a private search of the Phoenix, Marshall and Gilbert Island chains, as well as Tabiteuea and Christmas Islands, but turned up nothing. These private searches cost him a great deal of money. Acting on his attorney's advice, he became trustee of his wife's estate. By the time the prisoners were taken from the Hotel Kobayashi-Royokan, the last searches for them were over. ONI hoped the story of the century was about to blow over.

AUGUST 26, 1937

Guam, Mariana Islands

Captain Black was tying up to the wharf at Guam while the Man from ONI waited in his hot Washington office for some word from him. Kurt wasn't hopeful about getting information here. He was really just conducting business as usual as Guam was the point where he would pick up the goods that ONI had promised him. He went to his contact at Warehouse No. 2. to meet with Jim Cavanaugh, a pudgy little guy who reminded everyone of Peter Lorre. Kurt spotted him near some crates with a clipboard and asked, "What have you got for me, my friend?"

"Less than you think, I hope, you horny pirate," came the laughing reply.

Kurt smiled and retorted, "I'm sure it is, if you got your grabby little hands on it." They both laughed and went into his office where Jim grabbed a bottle of Flor-de-Cana, very smooth Nicaraguan rum that Kurt continually supplied.

"Did you bring me anything from Central America?" questioned the little man.

"Four cases, that ought to keep you happy, you little thief. And you call me a pirate?"

"Yes, I do, a horny pirate to be exact!"

They both sipped the smooth, light brown liquid and discussed the shipment that had come for Kurt. After enjoying another glass of rum, Jim led the way to the 12 crates that comprised the shipment. It was obvious they had all been opened.

"Did you get everything thing you wanted from my shipment?" Kurt inquired.

"No, but not everything I wanted was there."

"Thief!" Kurt exclaimed.

"Pirate!" Jim shot back.

Kurt went outside and signaled to four members of his crew to haul the booty back to his ship. He gave the bill of lading to his first mate and told him to check everything closely. The young Hawaiian nodded and quietly gave orders to the other three men who began prying open the crates.

"What's your next port of call?" Jim asked

"Probably Saipan with a stop at Rota. Why? Are you writing a book?"

"You might have problems at Saipan. I'm told they are a little, shall we say, paranoid lately. They weren't allowing the natives to leave the island since late July. It has hurt business here. You know the Japs, though. They see a spy around every corner."

"Hmmm, very interesting, I hope they still want to do business."

"With what you have in this shipment, I would say so, but you never know."

Kurt watched him head back to his office, probably for another shot of rum. His crew had placed the four cases of rum next to his desk. Suddenly Kurt's interest was piqued. He had dealt with the Japanese long enough to know that they reacted less than favorably to anything out of the ordinary. He stroked his chin and he thought. "I wonder what has got them all up in arms. Could it be a certain lady pilot?" He was already counting the money from the sale of his black market items and he used a key to open the strong box that his first mate had just handed him. Yes, ONI was good to their word: the box contained 2000 dollars in old ten dollar bills. This would be small potatoes if he uncovered Earhart's whereabouts. He left his crew to finish the loading and he went to the nearest bar with what today are described as "customer friendly bartenders". He stepped up to the bar and ordered a beer from the bare-chested bronze barmaid, with her colorful flower covered-panties and long, shiny black hair flowing down her back.

"Misser Firestone, what you want?" she asked with a sly smile.

"You if at all possible. But if not, a beer."

"Maybe both depend." Again, the sly smile.

"On what?" came his nothing ventured, nothing gained query.

"What you have to offer? I heard about you, you not......stay anywhere long." She looked up at him as she popped the cap off the bottle and handed it to him.

"That's right, but I'm a lot of fun while I'm around." He smiled or rather leered.

She laughed and bounced to the other end of the bar where two natives were just seating themselves. Kurt was always on the make and would usually stop whatever he was doing to make his pitch to a pretty girl. Sex was extremely important to him. But, it was obvious to everyone who knew him that only one thing was more important: and that was business. Business usually meant excitement, which meant an adrenalin rush and like it or not, it was his drug of choice. He smelled blood in the water with this Japanese shutdown of Saipan and he felt high.

By 2:30 in the morning he had shadowed every bar on the waterfront and found himself back across the bar from the bronze beauty with the flowered panties. He thought, I love her perfect boobs. He had gathered a lot of information, but nothing definitive about what was going on at Saipan. There were vague rumors and unfortunately for them both, nothing he could sell the Man from ONI.

"What are your plans for the next few days?" he asked.

"I have no plans. Maybe you tell me what is good?" Her smile was very inviting.

"I'm on my way to Saipan, want to go along?"

"NO, I got no reason to see Yapnese, they not nice!" Her dark brown eyes flashed.

"How about tonight? A trip to my ship?"

"Not go to ship with you, might find myself in Saipan tomorrow. You come to my place if you want, depend on how much you pay for beer."

Kurt threw down a five dollar bill for the twenty cent beer and got a nod in return. She closed up the bar and they both walked to her small apartment over a butcher shop near the waterfront. It was very cozy and decorated in bright colors, cane, rattan and beaded dividers for a door: a typical Guamanian home. She lost no time getting out of the panties she wore. Kurt didn't wait for a formal invitation. He scooped up her five-foot petite body that couldn't have weighed more than 95 pounds and whisked her to the bed in the corner of the one room flat. Saipan and ONI could wait a day or two. This one was a real live wire.

Two days later he was 10 miles out of Tannapag Harbor when he was stopped by a Japanese patrol boat and boarded. The young sub-lieutenant in charge was very aggressive and not in the mood for Kurt's explanation of why he was headed for Tanning Harbor. "Contact Commander Yamashita and ask him if I can come ashore." His Japanese was not very good, but the mention of Commander Yamashita got the desired results. The sub-lieutenant hot-footed it back to his patrol boat and five minutes later he barked orders to his men to get back aboard the Japanese patrol boat. As he pointed the boat towards the harbor, Kurt smiled his approval. It worked every time. Bullies always had to bow down to someone else higher in the hierarchy and he enjoyed the look on their faces when they had to wave him through. He was quarantined on board his ship the following day, the 29th of August, and it was the next morning before he was allowed off his ship. He was cordially greeted when he was escorted to Commander Yamashita's office. Kurt was delighted to see that the commander served him a drink of sake. That meant the Canadian Club was gone. Business would be good this trip!

Old Japanese jail, Garapan, Saipan.

CHAPTER SIXTEEN

AUGUST 29, 1937

Garapan Prison, Garapan, Saipan

Amelia and Fred arrived at the prison bound and blindfolded feeling the heat of the early afternoon. The stench of unwashed bodies, blood and filth assaulted their senses as soon as the vehicle pulled inside the walls. The uncomfortable ropes and blindfolds that dug into their now tender flesh were removed before they were shoved into their new lodgings. The cells were dirt-floored and the crumbling stucco walls were adorned with roaches and centipedes. Old rust-encrusted bars reached ceiling to floor acted as a front barrier between the guards' walkway and the cells. This, in effect, left zero privacy for any personal functions. The still, moldy air was disturbed only by a soaking tropical rain that provided both a blessing and a curse to the unfortunate inhabitants. They would receive a welcome cleansing shower, but had to sleep on wet straw and slop through the mud to their cor-ner "toilet" bucket each time it rained. The yard was a scene out of Dante's inferno, truly a hell on earth. The Saipanese, Guamanians and other native inmates were being starved. Obvious signs were apparent: hollow eyes, protruding ribs, boney and stick-like arms and legs. Many showed open wounds from numerous beatings, black eyes and missing fingers and toes. Everyone they saw was filthy beyond belief. Amelia and Fred feared that they would soon resemble this motley group.They were kept in separate cells and were allowed limited contact with each other and other captives. The diet, mainly unripe starchy bread-fruit, didn't agree with either of them and they didn't eat very much for four days after arriving. They realized that the breadfruit was better than starving to death so they finally began to eat. There were unidentified things thrown into the breadfruit, but they both picked them out and threw them in the pail that served as a toilet. The prisoners were allowed out of their cells to dump the buckets and have a few minutes in the sun. Amelia learned early on to put the pail in a corner at night to keep the rats from turning it over as they sought food.

The torture came once a week, every Friday. She would be walked to the interrogation room by a guard, who as time went on became less aggressive and threatening. Guerrero liked to interrogate the 200 odd prisoners on a regular schedule at night.

He knew that the screams would keep the entire population awake listening to the pain that would soon be their own. Amelia screamed less and less. She was withdrawing into herself.

Guerrero confided with his junior officer that morning before his ritualistic meeting with the unfortunates. "If I kill that bitch, the Commandant will have my skin. If I don't extract the information, he will have my skin. She's smart, so if I cut off fingers or toes she'll know we aren't going to let her go. Then she will never talk. If I inflict enough pain to make her hurt until the next session I feel sure that will wear her down, eventually. She'll talk, they all do." His subordinate just nodded, not knowing what to say.

She was a prize. The Japanese Naval Secret Police didn't want to answer to the hierarchy if she couldn't be released in order to enhance their country's world image. Amelia's master torturer inflected less pain on her than he did on other inmates. The others were, after all, only Guamanians, Saipanese and other islanders whose lives meant no more than the lives of the rats that made this prison home. The Americans' high status made them special and soon Guerrero stopped physical torture on a regular basis and leaned almost entirely towards mental agony. At random times he would surprise them with an impromptu interrogation for a surprise hour of anguish. Many factors compounded the agony Fred and Amelia endured on a daily basis. So, by October when the months of one meal a day cut into three parts and the dysentery had taken their toll, the pair was reduced to mere broken-spirited, filth-encrusted walking skeletons.

Prison life is terrible for very intelligent and accomplished individuals. It becomes repetition ad nauseam. Each day is replicated over and over until boredom and lack of productivity start to bring on a touch of madness. Time grinds on, but without measure, and the days run together into weeks and finally months. At night sleep becomes close to impossible while listening to the screams of the other prisoners, prisoners unlucky enough to be in the company of Guerrero. At first it was difficult to sleep during the day in the still, fetid air of the cell, but after a while it was possible due to exhaustion. The disgusting meals never varied and arrived precisely at the same time each and every day. The time in the yard was the same duration at the same time every day, week after week, month after month. The inside of the cell looked the same, only the bold, disgusting crawling and slithering creatures changed. Fred and Amelia were always there physically, trapped with their own personal stench of excrement and unwashed bodies. They never became accustomed to their environment, but they often left it all far behind by dreaming day and night of past pleasures and comforts. By the end of October Amelia resigned herself to the fact that she would never be rescued by any American cavalry riding over the hill.

When Guerrero had taken great glee in her humiliation last Friday by undressing her in front of a full length mirror, her depression was compete. He never sexually abused her; that would have aroused anger. His goal was to break her spirit. The image of her in the mirror was almost too much for her to endure. She weighed less than 70 pounds and her legs were now the size of her always slender arms. Her breasts and buttocks were practically non-existent. All her ribs were visible and her face was gaunt. There were bald spots on her head where hair had fallen out in great clumps. Her teeth were getting loose due to vitamin deficiency and her arms, legs, neck and back were full of the scars from Guerrero's "questioning".

It was as bad for Noonan, because special attention was given to his head injury. The subdural bleeding that had caused his horrible headaches was supposedly cured, but replaced with a gaping head wound that Guerrero made sure was always open and weeping. Noonan talked to Amelia less and less when they met in the yard, and she took little note of him as time passed. She had given him as much of her strength as she could and he had survived as a result. As with all situations like this, one must withdraw aid when one's own survival is at stake. By the last of October they had become just like the prisoners that had so appalled them when they first arrived at the "Garapan Hilton" But, the tiniest micro thin thread of hope still existed and an ember of defiance still glowed.

SEPTEMBER 9, 1937

ONI Headquarters, Washington, D.C.

Captain Black had made his visit to Saipan on the 1st of September as the Japanese had opened up travel to and from the island in late August. Not much of a problem for them because the two missing Americans were securely locked up in the Garapan Jail. Kurt had found out very little during his visit, but enough was implied to make him send ONI a message after he had informed Serge in Tokyo of his findings. The message was short but not very sweet.

COVEY PLUS ONE BELIEVED TO BE
ALIVE AND IMPRISONED ON SAIPAN.
NO DIRECT CONFIRMATION OF THIS
WAS AVAILABLE BUT CONVERSATIONS
WITH THE NATIVES WERE CUT SHORT
WHEN COVEY WAS MENTIONED.
ONE INDIVIDUAL TALKED ABOUT
TOKYO ROSA BUT THAT IS ALL I GOT.
I VENTURE TO SAY THEY ARE THERE
AND NOT GOING ANYPLACE. I WILL
CONTINUE TO WORK, SEND SUPPLIES.
BRIBES COSTING MORE EACH DAY.
DON'T EXPECT MUCH LUCK.
 CAPTAIN BLACK

Lanning read the message from Black and realized that this presented a new wrinkle to the growing Earhart problem. The few well informed individuals in the administration were at a loss. They didn't dare provoke the Japanese by demanding her release or even letting on that they knew she was in their hands. The Sino-Japanese war was in full swing and U.S. citizens didn't want to be dragged into another foreign war like the last one: horrible WWI memories still haunted Americans. They couldn't possibly leak news that Earhart was still alive and held by the

Japanese. That would require the administration to take overt actions to free her and the state of the military wasn't up to such an undertaking. On the other hand, if it did get out later that Washington knew about her predicament and did nothing, it would be political suicide for anyone involved. This information would be forwarded to the Assistant Chief of the Bureau of Navigation and he would inform the proper people in the White House. They would make the decision on what to do. He hoped.

OCTOBER 28, 1937

Garapan Prison, Saipan

It was the last week of October when Guerrero got the one piece of information he thought would crack Amelia's iron-like determination. It was a photograph of a document made by a Japanese spy in the Los Angeles County Court House. It had been secreted to Lieutenant Commander Yoshida at the Molino Roja (Red Mill) brothel in Tijuana, Mexico by a courier and forwarded to Tokkeitai Headquarters on Saipan.

He was itching to show it to her on Monday when he had received it, but waited until Thursday, because he had interrogated her just yesterday. Guerrero was very careful to use every little thing he had to wear down her spirit. He couldn't resist the temptation to gloat. This might be the mightiest blow to her yet in their battle of wills!

Amelia was startled when her guard came to get her on Thursday. This was too soon, she thought gloomily. What's going on? I don't know if I can take much more. She stood, head half raised and that took all the energy she had.

"I have something that you might like to see. You think they will come after you, so you will not tell us what we want to know. They have given up on you, the Americans and now……" His voice trailed off as he handed her the photograph. She didn't notice the smirk on his face.

Her mouth dropped open and her knees started to buckle as she strained to read the paper in the poorly lit room. George Putnam, her husband, had petitioned the Los Angeles County Court to have her declared LEGALLY DEAD. The words leaped off the page and hit her between the eyes. He had not only given up the search, but he was trying to get the seven year waiting period waived so he could take over managing her estate as soon as possible. Her chest tightened and she felt an oppressive weight crushing her physically and emotionally. The Japanese had been peeling her like an onion for what seemed like an eternity. The strong, defiant and independent woman, who omitted obey from the traditional matrimonial promise, now felt totally defeated. The small ember of hope burning inside her was snuffed out.

"You will now tell me where the films are. They have given up on you, why do you not tell me what I want to know?" He railed on at her getting a little red in the face.

"I don't know anything about films." She managed this answer because somewhere deep down inside side she still felt ONI might be able to recover the films.

"They have deserted you. Why do you persist in lying about the film?"

"I don't know what you're talking about."

"GET HER OUT OF HERE, NOW!" he shouted, losing his temper.

The Japanese guard led her back to her cell. She was like a zombie, unseeing, unfeeling, devoid of hope, and the light in her eyes was no more than a flicker. She didn't mention this latest development to Fred when she saw him in the yard two days later. He wouldn't have known what she was talking about anyway as Guerrero had been especially brutal during Noonan's latest questioning.

Amelia Mary Earhart Putnam died in her sleep two weeks later on November 13, 1937. Guerrero had tried during the last week to keep her alive, but without success: he had summoned the doctor who had put her in the Japanese hospital; he had left her completely alone, eliminating any torture, mental or physical; she was cleaned up; and he increased and improved her meals, but she had stopped eating. Despite his last-ditch efforts she had spent every day staring straight ahead at the walls of her cell and later the hospital room. She had completely lost the will to live.

Early the next morning, she and Noonan were taken by truck to the Catholic cemetery at Liyang. Her "funeral" took place one mile south of the prison near the quarry and the lumberyard. Guerrero had chosen two Saipanese guards and six prisoners to join the party. The prisoners dug two graves side by side while the guards looked on. Noonan, too weak to get out of the truck on his own, sat in the front corner of the truck bed, staring listlessly. After completing their unpleasant task, the prisoners retrieved Amelia, now wrapped in a sheet, and laid her in one of the graves while Noonan looked on. The prisoners were ordered back to the truck. Noonan knew what was going to happen and something deep inside welcomed an end to the suffering. He didn't hear the shot that Guerrero fired into the back of his head and he fell next to the open grave. The six men were herded back to the grave-sites from the truck. Guerrero had been careful to conceal the whole episode. No one saw him execute Noonan and within a half hour Noonan had been laid in the empty grave, both holes were filled in and no grave markings were left behind. The six inmates would be kept isolated and shortly hanged "for trying to escape." Guerrrero's carefully thought out plan went as expected. That is, except for the unnoticed pair of eyes hidden in the jungle bordering the cemetery that watched the entire event, including their departure.

DECEMBER 4, 1937

ONI Headquarters, Washington, D.C.

Lanning had notified the Assistant Chief of Navigation who had in turn notified the White House Representative. The President was still celebrating his election victory last month and was no longer concerned with Amelia Earhart. Pressing the Japanese government for the release of the two individuals was not going to happen. Too much of the capabilities of the Navy in the region would be laid open to conjecture and that would eventually lead to an investigation. At the very least, Captain Black's role in ONI's intelligence gathering network would be exposed. At worst, the Japanese government would guess that the U.S. was monitoring their radio transmissions and locating their ships using High Frequency Direction Finders. These were top secret operations and their disclosure or possible compromise was quite out of the question. It looked like nothing could be done to recover Earhart or her navigator. Their loss was just a casualty of world politics; a shame, but a fact of life.

The next best cover-up solution entailed doing absolutely nothing but repeating their previous cover stories and just letting the whole incident die down on its own. Naturally, this was the course of action decided on by the White House, and in turn, ONI. The president insisted that the situation should be continually monitored for any news of her, but the fact that she was still alive was being kept most confidential. It wasn't until January 9th of 1938 that word was received from Black that rumor had it that Earhart and Noonan had either been deported to Japan or executed. Black favored the latter, but couldn't be sure. He indicated in his message that he could do nothing more. What he didn't tell ONI was his contact in Tokyo, Sorge, had no information on Earhart or Noonan and if anybody should have the scoop, he would. Black went on with his 20th century swashbuckling pretty much unmolested. He would provide ONI with a very timely and important piece of information late in 1940, because he had uncovered the plan to bomb Pearl Harbor: he even had the day, a Sunday in December, but not the exact date. This important information would be lost or simply ignored: but that is a story best told at a later time.

Lanning was transferred to Tokyo as a military attaché before the end of 1937. He left the entire file on Operation Covey with his commander. It was marked "TOP SECERT/ POLITICALLY VERY SENSITIVE" The term Politically Very Sensitive meant White House involvement. It would be reviewed periodically by ONI as the situation developed. He hoped it wouldn't. In Tokyo, he would personally be on the lookout for any information regarding Amelia, but as usual cover-ups never ended, they just expanded as necessary.

Captain Chester W. Nimitz would become the commander of Cruiser Division Two, Battle Force in

April of 1938. Later he would take charge of Battle-ship Division 1, Battle Force in September of that year. On June 15th 1939 he would return to The Bureau of Navigation as its Chief. This promotion was only a segment of his meteoric rise to a Four Star Admiral and Commander of the Pacific Fleet on December 17th 1941. Four Stars in 18 months and two days wasn't bad for the grandson of a seaman in the German Merchant Marine. His grandfather taught him when he was young that "The sea-like life itself – is a stern taskmaster. The best way to get along with either is to learn all you can, then do your best and don't worry- especially about things over which you have no control."

George Palmer Putnam Sr. officially declared Amelia dead on January 5, 1938 and married Jean-Marie Cosigny James on May 21st, 1938. He published Amelia's biography, Soaring Wings in 1939. Later, he published Amelia's book, Round the World Flight, which he changed to *The Last Flight by Amelia Earhart*, taken from her periodic journal entries that she had sent back to him during her trip.

In the first week of November, 1937 the Japanese sent the *Kitkami* to Gardner Island in an attempt to find the missing film magazines. On the initial recon the *Kitkami's* seaplane crashed trying to land on the reef in approximately the same location the *Electra* had landed. The pilot misjudged the depth of the water and the float caught on the bottom. The biplane nosed over and flipped over on its back, killing the pilot and severely injuring the observer. The captain ordered as much of the aircraft that was usable to be salvaged while a shore party searched the island in vain for the much sought after film. The engine and floats and gear were salvaged, but most of the fuselage and the upper wing of the aircraft were left to be washed away by the surf. Although Captain Matsuyama felt the aircraft would be washed away before it was discovered, he took the trouble to make certain it couldn't be identified as Japanese. His men removed the lower wing with its red circles trimmed in white, the data plate and all cockpit instruments. He was pressured by his superiors to be very discreet. The Tokkeitai feared that a virtual spotlight would be focused on the island if he were to be spotted by the Americans or the British. Then, the U.S. Navy might search the island thoroughly if they thought the Japanese Navy was interested. The Japanese were extremely lucky, because the English expedition lead by Harry Maude landed on the island on the 13th of October, three weeks before the Japanese seaplane incident, to gauge its suitability for colonization. They found it acceptable and planned a colony which was started on December 20, 1938 with the arrival of the first colonists. The wreckage of the plane remained for several years after the island was colonized.

Earhart and Noonan haunted the dreams of the Japanese Tokkeitai, as they feared that the films the two had made of Truk Atoll could possibly be discovered by the Americans or British at some point in the future. The Roosevelt Administration feared that word would leak out that the Lockheed *Electra* wasn't at the bottom of the ocean, but probably in a hangar on Saipan or some other Pacific paradise. Kurt Feuerstein, Captain Black, was irked by his failure to get verified information on the location and fate of the pair. George Palmer didn't seem to suffer guilt or fear. His life was continuing on at a good pace. His marriage to Amelia seemed like a distant memory. One day in the future the President and ONI would find out that maybe Amelia and Fred's graves were not deep enough and the cover-up might just surface at the worst possible time. Maybe like long-lost relatives surprising newly blessed lottery winners at their secret celebration.

*Robert Wallack discovered Amelia's
briefcase on Saipan-1945.*

CHAPTER SEVENTEEN

JULY 9, 1944

Saipan, Mariana Islands

It was 4:15 in the afternoon, 7 years to the day since the USS *Colorado* had searched Garner Island and failed to find any trace of Amelia, Fred or the Lockheed *Electra*, when Admiral Turner declared Saipan officially secure. The 30,000-man Japanese Imperial Army's 43rd division commanded by Lieutenant General Yoshitsugu Saito had been virtually annihilated. Saito, all his subordinate commanders and Vice Admiral Chuichi Nagumo, who had commanded the carrier forces at Pearl Harbor and Midway, all committed suicide at the end of the battle. The victors were the Army's 27th Division, a New York National Guard unit federalized in 1940. Also, the 2nd and 4th Marine Divisions collectively suffered losses of 786 officers and 13,438 enlisted men killed, wounded and missing in action.

In late July CPT Jack Smith, a Marine Corps intelligence officer, made a startling discovery while interviewing Josephine Blanco, a Saipanese native. She freely related a story about "Tokyo Rosa", an American spy, that had been captured after her plane crashed near Chico Airbase at Tannapag Harbor in mid-1937. Smith was incredulous at first because he knew of only one American woman lost in the Pacific in 1937 and she had crashed at sea! He began to question her very closely about details of the incident. Josephine gave him the names and whereabouts of several Saipanese who had information about the incident.

Smith found out early on in his mission that the Saipanese were quite willing to talk to him. They had realized that the Emperor had lied about the horrible deaths that awaited them if they surrendered to the Americans. They had all been relocated into Camp Susuped (for Japanese Civilians) and Chalan Kanoa (all other local residents) where the conditions were primitive, but they were well-fed and not tortured as they had expected. At least 1,000 Japanese civilians had taken advantage of the Emperor's promise that any civilian who committed suicide would have an equal status in the hereafter as a soldier who died in battle. The Japanese POW's also expected to be tortured and die horrible deaths, but were more hesitant to open up until the American interrogators began to make them feel guilty for surrendering instead of dying in battle. The camp housed over 19,000 civilians by the end of the war. Although Smith had a monumental job, interviewing the almost 5500 Chamorros (Native Saipanese), Koreans and Carolina Island natives, his job turned out to be relatively easy. One stumbling block was that the islanders were fearful of a certain group of islanders and refused to talk to about past events. Jose Guerrero, the torturer, ex-prison guards and ex-island policemen still had intimidation powers over the other islanders. They presented a problem to Smith and his section.

The revelations by the Saipanese would have been shelved as hearsay by Smith and his section if not for the actions of Lance Corporal Robert Wallack on August 1, 1944. The young marine walked into headquarters carrying an attaché case and talked to Gunnery Sergeant Withers about what his team had found during the battle of Saipan.

"Gunnie, I brought in this case we found in a safe in the Japanese headquarters building.

"What's in it private?"

"A whole bunch of papers and…"

"Is it in Japanese?" interrupted the Gunnery Sergeant.

"No Gunnie, it's all in English and it's from Amelia Earhart."

"What the hell…" The sergeant's voice trailed as he snatched the case from Wallack and opened it.

"Oh my God…" His mouth gaped open. "Oh my God," was all he could manage."

He glanced at Wallack and motioned for him to sit down. He closed the case and quickly walked to Captain Smith's office.

"Sir, there's something you gotta see, it's…well… it's impossible but it's real."

"Gunnie, you look like you've seen a ghost, what could possibly be so important?"

"Take a look for yourself sir," Withers laid the case down on Smith's desk and opened it.

"Bunch of papers. It will be weeks before we can get them translated."

"Take a closer look sir."

Smith picked up one of the passports and opened it. His mouth opened and closed repeatedly as no words came out for a full minute. "Oh my God, this is all stuff from Earhart……and my god this is Noonan's…maps, country clearances, and charts. Jesus, where is the guy who got his hands on this?" He asked, rummaging through the case.

"At my desk, sir."

"Bring him in here, now!

"Aye, Aye sir."

Wallack was ushered into Smith's office where he snapped to attention and barked. Lance Corporeal Wallack reporting!"

"At ease Wallack, where the hell did you get this case?"

"I'm in charge of a machine gun section and we were detailed to take the headquarters building in the Jap compound. I found a safe that wasn't opened, so I ordered the demolitions guys to blow it and this was the only thing inside."

"Wallack, you've done well but this is a classified matter. Don't talk about it to anybody including the men in your section, understood?"

"Aye, Aye, sir!"

"If we need anything further, we'll get back to you."

"Aye, Aye, sir." Wallack turned and left the room.

Later, when Withers had gone Smith pulled a file, "Earhart Stories", from his desk and opened it. He started to read the interviews and thought this is big, really big; better getting to work on it ASAP. By the middle of August, Smith's section had put together the story of Amelia's and Fred's imprisonment on Saipan. It was early in the second week of August when he talked to Ben Silas who was a carpenter at the Japanese Chico Naval Base in 1937. He owned the pair of eyes that had witnessed the entire "funeral" drama at the Catholic Cemetery at Liyang, Saipan. He and his best friend told Smith the same story in separate interviews. Both were very, very fearful of Guerrero and his men who seemed to have a stranglehold on the island no matter who was in power. Smith took it upon himself to investigate the allegations made by the two men.

On August 15th, 1944 Smith took a truck and drove to Liyang cemetery. Enroute he picked up four men at a worksite just inside the main gate and in 20 minutes he pulled up outside the graveyard. Using a hand drawn map given to him by Silas, he led the work detail to the location indicated. Smith instructed the men to dig up the two graves very carefully as bones would be fragile. Graves Registration had provided two six-inch diameter metal tubes and within the hour the bones from two graves were safely inside. Marine Private Jim Saunders asked, "Who were these people?"

Smith replied, "They belong to a famous female aviatrix and her navigator!"

"Amelia Earhart?" questioned the young private.

"None other!"

The men in the detail put the tubes and shovels

on the truck and climbed aboard without another word.

"You men realize that this is not to be discussed with anyone, not even amongst yourselves."

"Aye, Aye, sir!" They all replied, almost in unison.

"This is a classified mission, period."

"Aye, Aye, sir!" Again, almost in unison.

Marine privates did exactly what Marine captains told them to do, just like they do today.

AUGUST 21, 1944

Headquarters, 27th Infantry Division
Saipan, Mariana Islands

Major James Lukshin, an Intelligence officer in the Division headquarters, had uncovered a very important piece of evidence located in a hangar at the southern end of the base. This information was gleaned by questioning many Japanese POW's and workers from the Chico Airbase. At first he had not believed what the low-ranking supply clerk from the base had said. The young Japanese private was too scared to take his own life and now was afraid to talk to the American major. Major Lukshin was a very experienced interrogator and played on the young man's fears of being tortured for information.

"We have no reason to spare anyone who doesn't cooperate with us. Are you going to cooperate, Private?" Lukshin asked and fixed him with his steel-like gaze. The Emperor had warned them previously about how barbaric the Americans were to captured soldiers.

"I am...am on...ly a...a...aa low...ly clerk. Wh.. wa...wahhh...at could I know?" stuttered the young man trying hard to control his fear.

"Something that will make us want to keep you alive and in one piece," again Lukshin bored holes in the young soldier with his piercing blue eyes.

"Theeeere issss a, a civv...ilian air, aircraft in Han...gar number 12" The young man was stuttering so badly the interpreter could hardly understand him.

"So what?" came Lukshin's clipped retort to the clerk's reply.

"No...oottt Jap...an...Japanese, Ahh...American." Again, the interpreter had a hard time understanding him.

Lukshin was somewhat taken aback. "How did it get here?" He pressed.

"Tha...that...is allllll I,I ka..know. Pleee..please don't tor...tor...torture me, please."

"Get the sniveling bed wetter the hell out of here!"

The two guards took the young clerk to the back door of the building which opened onto the compound and pushed him through it. Several older prisoners looked on without changing expressions. When the guards got back, Major Lukshin ordered. "Get us a jeep, Corporal Johnson! We need to find Hanger 12 ASAP!"

"Yes sir!" barked Johnson as he hurried out of the room. He returned 10 minutes later. "The jeep is ready, major!"

"Let's get on with it then." A wry smile formed on Lukshin's face, the smile of someone who knows something no one else does. He then thought to himself, the sonofabitch cracked like an egg dropped on the sidewalk.

One half later Major Lukshin and Corporal Johnson cut the lock on Hangar 12 and went inside. The flashlights they had borrowed from the yard foreman weren't necessary because part of the roof was missing and the afternoon sun provided enough light. They walked to the back southwest corner of the damaged building filled with dead foliage and bird nests and there it was! Lukshin pulled the stubby, unlit cigar he constantly chewed from his mouth and threw it to the ground. He knew he was looking at NR16026 even before he looked under the wings to verify it. This was AMELIA EARHART'S PLANE! The twin-ruddered Lockheed *Electra* was unmistakable. It was a little worse for wear. The tires were flat, but it actually looked flyable! His heart was beating like a jack hammer when he said, "We need a camera, and we need it now!"

"But sir, no pictures are allowed in……"

"NOW, JOHNSON! Get me a fucking camera, NOW!!"

"Yes sir!" was the only acceptable reply as the corporal double-timed out of the hangar

AUGUST 31, 1944

ONI Headquarters, Washington, D.C.

Rear Admiral Roscoe E. Schuirmann, Chief of the Office of Naval Intelligence read the report from Saipan with both interest and consternation. He wondered how this could have happened? An army major and a marine captain had solved the mystery of the century: What happened to Amelia Earhart? He pulled out the file from his desk marked "TOP SECRET/POLITICALLY SENSITIVE and read it as the sickening feeling in his stomach grew with every word. Earhart's disappearance was seven years old and extremely old news in light of the fact that the most destructive event that humanity had conjured up to date was just drawing to a close. Something about "the lives of two people not amounting to a hill of beans" briefly invaded his thoughts. "Politically sensitive" meant that it was the privy of the White House. Schuirmann put all the paperwork into his briefcase and called the Chief of the Navy Bureau of Navigation for an appointment.

"Grace, would you get me the Chief at Navigation?"

"Yes sir, one moment."

"Thank you Grace. Would you ring me back?"

"Of course, sir."

Schuirmann read the file while he waited.

"The Chief is on the line sir."

"Thank you, Grace. Chief, Roscoe here, down at ONI."

"How's it going down there?"

"Good, but I need to talk with you about a sensitive matter."

"I'm awful busy, could it wait until tomorrow?"

"If you wish, but it's Top priority/Politically sensitive."

"Get over here as soon as you can."

"Yes sir."

His briefing of the Chief had just begun when the Naval Liaison for the White House joined them. Schuirmann gave his briefing in his usual clipped and professional manner and was thanked and basically dismissed. He was more than happy to get rid of this headache. Presidential involvement in any intelligence matter is sticky at best. This was especially true of this case, because he had inherited it from his predecessors. He was told to keep them informed and any instructions would be forthcoming.

When he left the meeting the presidential liaison said, "I was afraid of this. President Roosevelt is in a tough reelection campaign and here comes a missile from the distant past to blow up in his face. I will talk to him, but I can assure you he doesn't want any of this to come to light. I hope you understand that, Admiral?"

"Yes sir, I do, only too well. I will take action to divert any further investigation and do what I can to, shall we say, to make these reports go away."

"I think we understand each other, Admiral. Public knowledge of the president's involvement in this matter would be political suicide. It must be stopped now."

"I understand." Admirals do what presidents tell them to do."

SEPTEMBER 1, 1944

Chief, ONI Section, Saipan, Mariana Islands

The message was sent that same day by the Chief of ONI to the Chief of ONI on Saipan:

TOP SECRET

THE AIRCRAFT FOUND IN HANGER
12 AT CHICO NAVAL BASE IS TO
BE COMPLETELY DESTROYED. THE
REMAINS ARE TO BE COMBINED
WITH DEBRIS FROM DESTROYED
ENEMY MATERIAL AND BURIED IN
A CENTRAL DUMP. THE REMAINS
RECOVERED AT THE CEMETERY AT
LIYANG ARE TO BE SHIPPED BY THE
FASTEST MEANS POSSIBLE TO THIS
OFFICE. ANY OTHER INVESTIGATION

OF THIS MATTER IS TO BE CEASED
IMMEDIATELY AND THE ENTIRE
MATTER IS NOW CLASSIFIED TOP
SECRET. ALL INDIVIDUALS WHO HAVE
KNOWLEDGE ARE TO BE INFORMED
OF THIS NEW STATUS. RECIEPT OF
THIS IS TO BE ACKNOWLEDGED
IMMEDIATELY.
SIGNED
CHIEF OF OFFICE OF NAVAL INTELLIGENCE

TOP SECRET

Major Lukshin had the aircraft pulled from the hangar, doused with gasoline and burned. The engines were taken apart and broken up into smaller pieces. The engine serial numbers were removed with a cutting torch. Two sailors continued to douse the burning aircraft until only hunks of melted aluminum remained. The wreckage was taken to the main material disposal site and unceremoniously dumped along with the scrap metal from destroyed enemy equipment. Captain Smith personally put the metal tubes, the attaché case and all the records of the investigation on a special transport to ONI headquarters in Washington D.C. Both Lukshin and Smith went back to their duties knowing that something far above their pay grades was in the works and keeping quiet was the best thing they could do.

. . . .

ONI Headquarters was operating at full speed and full capacity. The recent successes of the invasions of Saipan, Tinian and Guam were being overshadowed by preparations for a big push into the Japanese Home Islands. There wasn't a lot of time to gather intelligence on a little island that was to become a reality for the militaries of both the United States and Japan. Japan had lost all hope of winning the war with the loss of the Marianas. They had developed a new strategy, one of dogged defense of every last inch of their home territory. If the Allies were going to conquer Japan, they were going to pay dearly for it. There was no shortage of men, women and children willing to sacrifice their lives in the defense of their Emperor and their homeland. Iwo Jima would be where Japan started her last stand. The United States realized that this wasn't going to be easy. The Allied Powers had decided on unconditional surrender, leaving the Japanese with no choice but to fight until they were totally annihilated.

The evidence of Amelia's and Fred's demise at the hand of the Japanese couldn't have hit the Roosevelt administration at a worse time. The election campaign of 1944 was drawing to a close. It was the eleventh hour and the opposition was looking for a way to slam the Democrats. Amelia was that large hammer. The president and his advisers could just see the headlines: "ADMNISTRATION DESERTS EARHART IN HER HOUR OF NEED."; "JAPS KILL AMELIA, ROOSEVELT DOES NOTHING."; "HE SOLD AMELIA OUT, WILL HE SELL US OUT TOO?" And then there were the cartoons to come. They would be brutal at best. There was no choice but to bury Amelia and Fred for good. The president had his eye on the re-election campaign of 1948 when he would try for a fifth term and revelations of the fate of the pair would do no one any good. Everyone in the White House agreed. Make it disappear; public knowledge will not benefit anyone. This seemed to be the party line. As it turned out FDR died of a cerebral hemorrhage on April 12, 1945, 83 days into his 4th term. Congress later passed a Constitutional Amendment limiting presidential terms to two.

Captain Jerry Jacobi was assigned to handle the mechanics of the case. He had been given his orders by Rear Admiral Schuirmann, "Bury the entire incident, as deep as possible!" The admiral had given the orders with very little emotion but a lot of emphasis. Jacobi was the right man for the job. He started by arranging for the burial of the two sets of remains. They would be given funerals with full military honors under assumed names, of course. He carefully went through every piece of paper that had been sent or received on the matter, including Wallack's attaché case. Each one was destroyed by him personally. Jacobi was assured of the silence of everyone in the intelligence community and the people on Saipan would have no reason to recall the incident. But, he had to make sure. He sent word to the commander of US Forces on Saipan that the island was to be closed to everyone, other than military personnel until further notice. By the time the pair was buried in early February of 1945, everything was in order except for two problems.

The man in charge of intelligence on the Marshall Islands, Captain George Bundy, had forwarded a suitcase that one of his men had found in a billet used by the Japanese. It was reported as having women's clothes and a diary bound in red leather, which bore the inscription, "The Diary of Amelia Earhart". The diary wasn't in the suitcase that had been received from Kwajalein. He had to keep the suitcase and all its contents until everything was accounted for. It was a loose end and Jacobi hated loose ends. Jacobi was later reassigned to the Naval Technical Training Unit (NTTU), a special intelligence operations section of ONI on Saipan. In March of 1946, the diary had been the object of a very thorough search with negative results. Jacobi destroyed the clothing, suitcase and paperwork from Kwajalein when it became apparent the diary wasn't going to be located.

The second problem arose while going through Wallack's attaché case. All the clearances, charts and correspondence associated with the flight were accounted for except there were no passports for either Earhart or Noonan. This, he thought was very strange, and sent a message to Captain Smith on Saipan. Smith answered "I don't remember seeing any passports in the case at the time."

The matter was finished: Amelia Mary Earhart Putnam and Frederick "Fred" Joseph Noonan were buried. The public had become accustomed to the story of them crashing into the sea on July 2, 1937. Everyone who had anything to do with the story or the cover-up had been taken care of. The native population on Saipan would be kept in check by the NTTU and the CIA until the 1960's. Every piece of evidence had been destroyed and all mention of the mission had been scrubbed from the records. Jacobi left his office almost entirely satisfied with the accomplishment of his mission, except for a nagging little voice that caused him to stop momentarily before leaving the building.

"WHAT THE HELL HAPPENED TO THE DIARY AND THE PASSPORTS?" He whispered to himself. He stood there thinking for a few seconds, shrugged his shoulders and left the building.

AUTHORS' NOTES

We wrote this book to try to logically explain what happened to Amelia and Fred. There are almost as many theories about her disappearance circulating as there are people who know the story. Many individuals have come forward and given testimony about her imprisonment on Saipan at the hands of the Japanese Empire. Many "experts" have tried to debunk theories that she was on a secret mission for the American government and that these witnesses are lying. Look at the testimony and realize that the Japanese had no reason to kidnap and imprison her if she hadn't photographed their secret installations. She had no reason to photograph their installations on her own, so who else would she have done it for? The Japanese have less reason today to admit they kidnapped her than they did in 1937. These are questions that need to be asked.

Although some of this book is fiction, much of it is also based on documented historical fact. Did the conspiracy we described actually exist? We don't know. We merely suggest that it could have existed and that she and Fred met their end as we have described. In many cases people and places are real and historically accurate, but we have taken liberties with their dialogue and their participation in events.

We wish to thank George Palmer Putnam, Jr., Amelia Earhart's stepson, and Marie Putnam, his wife. They welcomed us into their home, shared their treasured memories of Amelia and gave their kind permission to use several images from their collection.

We wish to extend our heartfelt thanks to Ms. Amy Wische, our agent. Without her skill at editing and proofreading this book wouldn't be in its present readable form. Ms. Wische also provided the encouragement throughout the entire process that kept us on track and focused. Without her this project wouldn't have made it past the first draft.

Finally we wish to thank our very patient families and friends, who have put up with our dedication to this project. They have happily acted as sounding boards and proofreaders and their advice has been invaluable. They realized, early on, that this was a tribute to Amelia and Fred for their contributions to aviation and the role of women and men in a free society. For many years people have lauded Amelia for her contributions in the advancement of women in our society. Fewer people realize that Fred Noonan was eager to work for Amelia, something that most men weren't receptive to then or even now.

For individuals who want further information about the technical data and factual information used in writing this novel please visit our website at **www.ameliaearhartcontroversy.com**. We welcome your comments.

CO-AUTHORS' BIOGRAPHIES

Robert "Bob" Wheeler is a retired Military and Civilian Helicopter and Airplane Pilot. He is a Certified Helicopter Instructor Pilot and an Instrument Flight Examiner. During Bob's 39-year military career he had combat tours in Vietnam, Desert Storm and Afghanistan and has done extensive research helping to locate Missing Helicopter Crews in Vietnam. His passionate research of the Amelia Earhart mystery dates back to 1967. Bob has combined his research ability, 38 years of aviation experience and many contacts in the aviation community to produce this first novel. Bob lives in Florida and West Virginia near his two daughters.

Harold "Fred" Nicely is a retired Military and Civilian Helicopter and Airplane Pilot as well as a Helicopter Instructor Pilot. During his 37-year military career, he completed an 18 month combat tour in Vietnam from1967-69. Fred's passion for aviation began while listening to stories his father, a waist gunner on a B17 during the war, told him as a child. He has studied the early aviation greats Rickenbacker, Lindbergh, Earhart and Post since those early days. Fred has enjoyed a 36-year aviation career where he developed his extensive research ability and knowledge of celestial navigation. This is his first novel. Fred lives in Ohio with his wife, Betty. His son followed in his footsteps as a Military Helicopter Pilot.

REFERENCE

NOTES

Paul L. Briand Jr., Requiem for Amelia, www.
broadcovemedia.com/Requiem_for_Amelia.pdf, 1967

Rick Gillespie, The Earhart Project, www.tighar.
org/Projects/Earhart/AEdescr.html, 2012, Various
contributions by various authors on a variety of
related subjects.

Gary LaPook, https://sites.google.com/site/
freddienoonan, 2012

http://www.lib.perdue.edu/spcol/aearhart/
collectiom/php

Wikipedia, http://en.wikipedia.org/wiki/Axial_
tilt#Measurement, 2012

OLE NIKOLAJSEN, http://www.ole-nikolajsen.com/navtales.htm, 2012

http://www.celestial-navigation-course.com/mainmenu/mainmenu0.php, 2012

http://en.wikipedia.org/wiki/E6B#History_of_the_E-6B, 2012

http://www.csgnetwork.com/e6bcalc.html, 2012

http://en.wikipedia.org/wiki/Edwin_T._Layton, 2012

http://tighar.org/Projects/Earhart/Archives/Research/ResearchPapers/Worldflight/finalflight1.html, 2012

http://www.hnsa.org/doc/ecat/cat-0642.htm, 2012

http://en.wikipedia.org/wiki/Horizon#Distance_to_the_horizon, 2012

http://earlyradiohistory.us/1963hw13.htm#13sec6, 2012

http://tighar.org/Projects/Earhart/Archives/Documents/Report_487/Report487.pdf, 2012

http://en.wikipedia.org/wiki/
File:Lockheed_12A_G-AGTL_Ringway_14.04.58_
edited-2.jpg, 2012

http://oceannavigation.blogspot.com/2009/01/
celestial-navigation-sun-line-running.html, 2012

http://www.aviation-history.com/engines/pr-1937.htm,
2012

http://www.sunrisesunset.com/predefined.asp,
2012

http://www.researcheratlarge.com/Pacific/RDF/,
2012

http://www.pagetutor.com/trigcalc/trig.html,
2012

http://www.wsanford.com/~wsanford/exo/sundials/
DEC_Sun.html, 2012

Gary La Pook, 5 May 2011, http://www.fer3.com/
arc/m2.aspx?i-116311&y=201104, 2012

http://tighar.org/Projects/Earhart/Archives/Forum/
Highlights101_120/highlights105.html, 2012

Randall S. Jacobson, Ph.D., http://tighar.
org/Projects/Earhart/Archives/Research/
ResearchPapers/Phoenixislands.html, 2012

http://tighar.org/Projects/Earhart/Archives/
Documents/Hooven_Report/HoovenReport.html,
2012

http://www.historywiz.com/historymakers/earhart.htm,
2012

REFERENCE

BIBLIOGRAPHY

Putnam, George P. *Last Flight by Amelia Earhart*,
New York, New York, 1937

Goerner, Fred, *The Search for Amelia Earhart,*
Doubleday and Company, Garden City, NJ 1966,
ISBN 0385074247/0-385-07424-7

Elgen M. Long and Marie K. Long, *Amelia Earhart,*
The Mystery Solved, Simon and Schuster,
Rockefeller Center, New York, NY 10020, 1999,
IBSN 0-684-86005-8

HONORING AMELIA EARHART

"She embodied the spirit of an America coming of age and increasingly confident, ready to lead in a quite uncertain and dangerous world."

Hillary Clinton, U.S. Secretary of State, in a speech March 20, 2012 in Washington D.C. to welcome scientists launching a new expedition to find the lost aviator, Amelia Earhart.

"She boosted the capabilities of trained and talented women."
"She was a competent lady...didn't get excited about little things."
"She was very knowledgeable in her field... a can do woman."

George Palmer Putnam Jr., stepson of Amelia Earhart, in an interview with the author at his home on March 27, 2012

"I want to tell you, Amelia Earhart and her navigator did go down in the Marshall Islands and were picked up by the Japanese."

WWII Fleet Admiral Chester A. Nimitz conveyed to CBS journalist, Fred Goerner in 1965